Sarah Houssayni is a Lebanese American writer, pediatrician, and mom. She is a clinical associate professor at Kansas University. Her narratives have published in Family Medicine, Survive and Thrive, The Examined Life, Pulse Voices, and St. Cloud Repository. She is a Reader's Digest Award winner for a personal essay; her novel *Fireworks* was a Chanticleer Book Award finalist. This is her second novel.

This book is for Maysaa and Johanna.

Sarah Houssayni

WASTED SALT

AUSTIN MACAULEY PUBLISHERS™

LONDON • CAMBRIDGE • NEW YORK • SHARJAH

Ordering Information:
Quantity sales: special discounts are available on quantity purchases by corporations, associations, and others. For details, contact the publisher at the address below.

Publisher's Cataloging-in-Publication data
Houssayni, Sarah
Wasted Salt

ISBN 9781643786544 (Paperback)
ISBN 9781643786551 (Hardback)
ISBN 9781645364733 (ePub e-book)

Library of Congress Control Number: 2019917070

www.austinmacauley.com/us

First Published (2020)
Austin Macauley Publishers LLC
40 Wall Street, 28th Floor
New York, NY 10005
USA

mail-usa@austinmacauley.com
+1 (646) 5125767

Iain and Noah: you inspire me, encourage me, mend my heart, and make every breath worth taking and every battle worth peacefully winning. I am blown away by your intellect, humbled by your hard work, and endlessly entertained by your humor. I love you with everything I got.

Nazih: my family since August of 1997. You got my back despite, against and regardless. I am so thankful and so blessed.

My family of birth: Mama, Rami, brothers, sisters, cousins, aunts, and uncles. The distance cannot erase the memories. Thank you for claiming me.

My family of choice: you make the home away from home just as sweet and just as warm. That includes you too, Wonder Twin, like you say "WE ARE KING!"

My first readers: this story is because you asked for more.

Charles: what a teacher, what a friend. Thank you for every email, every advice, and every encouragement.

Meghan: your faith in me makes me try harder. Thank you for always reading what I write, thank you for being the kind, loving friend you are.

Grayson: thank you for editing my manuscript.

Juno: thank you for walking the walk and talking the talk. What an advocate!

Ronia Stephen: thank you for donating your time to model for the cover picture, you are as beautiful inside as you are on the outside.

Paula Moore: thank you for your great work with the cover photo.

Residents, colleagues, staff, students, and patients at the Via Christi Family Medicine Residency: you make the grief of sickness bearable, the joy of health bigger, and work not feel like a chore.

"Even in our sleep, pain which cannot forget
Falls drop by drop upon the heart
Until, in our own despair, against our will,
Comes wisdom through the awful grace of God."
— *Aeschylus*

Foreword

What you hold in your hand is a tribute. A tribute to the multiple powers of humanity. To the power of struggle to impact the course of life. To the power of friendship. To the power of resilience. To the power of transformation. To the power of changing places to find oneself. The power of home, in leaving it, and in loving it despite its imperfections, in finding it anew.

Here is the continuing story of Zahra. A stone tumbled in the waters of past war Beirut, where mortar shells live inside of the hearts, minds, bodies of people, and govern their decisions in large and small ways. Her life ripples out into the life of others showing the interconnectedness of small daily decisions, failures, triumphs, and accomplishments. As you wade through the waters of her stagnant and well-circumscribed life in Lebanon, you learn bit-by-bit about what has driven her to US—to Wichita Kansas no less.

Here you get to know Zahra, not as the young, sometimes petulant love-stricken teenager, resistant to norms and fascinated by her body's capacity she was in Sarah Houssayni's equally captivating *Fireworks*—but rather now as the determined, self-reliant, if ailing, adult she has become. What makes this story captivating and luscious though is the strong oceanic pull of the interwoven characters of Zahra's life, who defy the usual simple categorization even if they are personifications of type. Each character has volume and edges; they are tangible and lasting. They are also diverse.

We are brought into the world of Zahra's relationship through her contact Nadim, a physician who has a brotherly love for Zahra, a long-standing patient-physician relationship that has become more of mentorship and sponsor as he has helped support Zahra to recover physically and emotionally from war injuries. We learn of her quiet and contented relationship with Nadim's mother, Hajji, Zahra's elderly charge for whom Zahra cares for with grace, and who fills the space emotionally and economically her family would not.

And then there's Mustafa, Zahra's friend who, since childhood, has been determined to be a hairstylist, both typifying and exuberantly flushing out his identity as a flamboyant gay man living in Lebanon's superficially sexually restrictive landscape. His life is in contrast to so many others who feel constrained and unable to live out their dream. But, inspired in some way by Mustafa, Zahra pursues her dream of bodily restoration and psychic expansion of place and belonging, and goes to the US.

In a telling description of what it means to move and be moved by a new place, Zahra works to find ways to live and adjust in a new place where food, jobs, expectations, clothes, and even cleaning products are so different and often incomprehensible from what she is familiar with. But, as a keen observer of life, Zahra finds her path towards her goal of restoration despite, being largely tossed aside by family and would-be family in Lebanon.

In the U.S., Zahra finds herself and strength in an unconventional chosen family who accept and support her despite physical challenges, constraints, and cultural barriers.

Her chosen family is a bit of a motley crew, that once again brings forth the power of unbridled living despite systematic life challenges, and includes a Noor, who exemplifies womanhood even as hers is challenged, and Iris a woman of faith whose own struggles bring her to a practical positivity that supports Zahra in finding her way.

Here we see the power of humanity, of diversity of race, creed, color, language, and sexual orientation, and gender identity, to see the gritty, human, and often physically violent struggles people face to living as their authentic selves.

For this reason, I believe I was asked to write this forward. What Sarah Houssayni has done here is demonstrate the importance of seeing people…all people…for who they are at heart. Even when people are complicated and living in complicated situations, all need love, support, and healing.

As a physician and co-director of The PRIDE Study (pridestudy.org), a long-term study of sexual and gender minority people who include but is not limited to lesbian, gay, bisexual, queer, and transgender (LGBTQ+) people, I know that the realities of people's lives, as they are lived, are often invisible. But beyond that, often LGBTQ+ people face harsh discrimination, neglect, and acts of violence that threaten life, well-being and prevent the pursuit of dreams. Unfortunately because of this stigma and discrimination, LGBTQ+ people face numerous health challenges that are often magnified by trouble in seeking or obtaining appropriate health care. This is especially true for our most vulnerable folks and for people who have many overlapping identities: being immigrants or refugees, people of color, youth, and especially transgender people. *Wasted Salt* brings these struggles into high relief, amidst beautiful storytelling that draws you into people's lives only to realize upon stepping back the devastating impact of living a life that may not be legible to others, but is nonetheless, valiant, beautiful, and powerful!

Read on, enjoy, learn, dwell, and grow through reading the truth expressed in this novel. Then look to see how you can enhance what you do to make sure the beauty of ALL people's lives can be lived OUT loud in your family, hometown, communities, religious center, or school. By buying this novel you are supporting these efforts by donating to The PRIDE Study—thank you! I vow to use any proceeds to promote health and wellbeing of LGBTQ+ people. You can learn more about our efforts and other ways to help at our website. But, I challenge you to do more. I urge you to look inside yourself and your life and commit to helping us all realize a world of healing and growth where all people have a chance to realize their dreams free from war, free from hatred, free from discrimination, and free from misunderstanding. The power of this book is in seeing how you can make this possible through greater understanding. You and your actions can help us all straddle the bridge between our current reality and this more beautiful future. So, join me, take whatever steps you can to bring that sometimes-elusive future into being. That oh-so-beautiful future where all can live in full expression of their dreams may be much closer than you think, if we all take actions in our lives to make sure that no one's personhood or being-ness is considered "Wasted Salt."

Chapter One

"I am going to the Jama'a hospital, just let me out here," Zahra said.

She shut the red cab door harder than she meant to. A hot breeze met her on the side of the street, and it felt cooler than the jammed car with broken window handles and no air conditioning; Beirut transportation at its best.

Zahra looked for a good spot to cross the street. She needed to get to the other side to walk straight down to the hospital. She thought about the elderly woman with huge white bags in her lap. Zahra tried to give her room inside that cab. She stuck to the window and didn't move to make space for the woman and her things. The woman seemed old and tired of carrying heavy bags in a busy city. She was in the cab when Zahra got in, next to another passenger, one who Zahra couldn't see much of from the piled bags. When Zahra sat next to her, the woman smiled and moved the bags from the thick clear plastic covered seat to her lap, her hand was thin skin, brown spots, and bulging blue lines traveling to her crooked fingers.

"*Afwan,*" Zahra said, excusing herself. There was not much space for her to sit.

The woman smiled again under her mountain of things again when Zahra got out of the cab. Zahra nodded and made her exit quickly, unintentionally sending a loud, slamming door towards the old woman. She looked both ways before deciding to walk in the shade towards Wardiyeh Street.

A loud honk startled Zahra a few steps later. She saw her red cab stop down the street. The car behind it was initiating the sequentially louder honks, now in rhythm with the driver's arm waving out of the window. White bags arose from the back seat, held by a wiry arm.

The blaring of one horn gave way to a chorus of protesting bleats and a street full of angry drivers. Traffic was stopped. Zahra looked away. She pushed herself between two cars parked close together and crossed to the other side of the street. She hurried down the intersection and then down another street.

The faster she moved, the better the city digested the honks, until nothing was left of it but the usual rumbling of the monster's belly: whiny beggars, congested engines, hurried pedestrians.

Once she got to a shaded spot under a building, Zahra got her cell phone out to see if Nadim had texted her. He was probably busy, something came up—something always came up. He said he would come out of the clinic building and meet her at the doctor's café. She despised that place the worst, always some doctor, some nurse, some hospital employee who remembered taking care of her. Zahra ran her hand over her black T-shirt and traced the bag against her flesh. It was empty; she hoped it would stay empty until she was back at home.

Nadim was not in front of his clinic building. She considered waiting outside for him. The sun was thumping the sidewalk, making the bricks look bright and dry. The only shadow around was a tree, under which a woman was puffing her cigarette in long billowy swirls of white. She didn't look hurried to be done. Zahra stood by the steps watching her finish her smoke and flick its dwarfed end groundward onto the yellowed brick rectangles. The woman walked away from the still burning stub as Zahra walked towards it, an understanding slight nod between them as they passed one another. Zahra pulled out her phone again as she stepped on the cigarette and smashed it flat. He still hadn't texted her.

"*Ana natra,*" she typed, nothing else, to tell him besides the obvious. She hated waiting.

"*Shoo kifik?*" Nadim said. He appeared behind her with his usual smile. He always asked how she was before anything else.

"*Mniha,*" she replied. She was good, but also hot and sweaty.

He gestured to the doctor's café like he always did, and she followed him, slowly and reluctantly. This would be her last time to come see Nadim and follow him anywhere.

Nadim was a handsome and kind cardiologist. Patients, their families, and hospital employees flocked to him everywhere he went. Zahra watched him nod and wave with his tenacious smile. She looked away anytime some greeter's gaze went to her after him.

Many but not all hospital staff had seen her with him. It was what they didn't say that sounded the worst; she was neither family nor a friend, more like an obvious charity case. He always introduced her as "My little Zahra," even ten years after she was no longer sixteen. Zahra wished he didn't say anything about her. People didn't care to be introduced, and some of them had already met her making the prefatory show even more unnecessary.

The hospital's café was empty except for the volunteer lady in pink; "*Mrs. Nabila*" according to a silver nametag pinned a little sideways above her right breast. The occasional

16

clanking of pans and muffled voices were audible from the little kitchen behind Mrs. Nabila's black swivel chair. The lady in pink went back to her magazine after grinning her dentures at Nadim and Zahra, but mostly to Nadim. Nadim grabbed two juice bottles from the tall glass fridge and gestured Zahra to the back corner.

"It's hotter than hell today," he commented.

"What makes you think hell is hot?" she said. He smiled and she did too.

Nadim was the one who always told her those same words. It was her turn to throw his sarcasm back to him. He told her what he never told anyone else, she was his "project human," his Frankenstein.

They met in 2006, when she was sixteen and he was thirty. She was critically injured by a bomb dropped from an Israeli helicopter, he was a volunteer physician helping at the hospital she was transported to. The medics assessed her injury to be "incompatible with life" but Nadim did not agree. He insisted that she be sent to the operating room and donated two units of his own blood to make up the ten units she needed to stay alive. She lived and became his "protégée." He stayed around and became the unintentional object of her affection, attention, and thoughts. Over the ten years that she knew him, Nadim grew on her heart like vines on old brick buildings; impossible to remove.

"Are you packed?"

"Not much to put in a bag, I don't think I will take much," Zahra said.

"Well, if you forget something, don't be thinking I will be taking it to you! Wichita, Kansas, is farther than the moon," Nadim teased. He giggled at his joke.

Zahra nodded. She knew it was far. The few things she knew about Wichita: far, hot in the summer, and open for refugees like her. She planned on leaving her winter clothes behind. She needed to take as little as possible. Her mother would eventually give away the black sweaters, black pants, and black jacket, possibly to a woman in mourning over a dead family member.

Zahra looked around the café, for nothing in particular. She wanted their farewell done already. There was no sense in dragging it. Nadim said he would visit her in Wichita, he said he would call and email. She didn't want him to call and email her. She didn't want him to visit and then leave her.

She nodded and smiled occasionally. Her bottle of orange juice was empty now; she was cradling it in her hands, soaking up the vanishing chill from the glass.

"You need the list of numbers, make sure you have the list when you get a phone. Program the numbers into the phone, just like you do here. It will be a simpler phone, easier to operate," he said.

He had already told her twice and called her several times about everything she needed to do and have once she got to Wichita. His deliberate and insistent way in going over what she, at twenty-six, needed to do was infuriating. Her body was hurt but her mind was always fine.

She took a deep breath and looked at him. She could always escape him best when she got lost in his face. She knew where every line started and exactly where it ended. At forty, Nadim had started to get some gray in his short black hair. She knew when his hair got long enough for a haircut and what he would look like the day following one. It seemed to Zahra, at times, that she made him up in her many morphine-induced hallucinations and never figured out how to make him go away when she returned to reality.

"I was your age when I left for my residency," he commented.

"You were a year younger," Zahra asserted.

The story of Nadim leaving Lebanon after completing his medical school was etched in her mind. She knew it possibly better than Nadim himself. He was twenty-five. His mother and father took him to the airport on a Sunday morning and he has never really cared for Sundays ever since. It was June and the sun was just coming out. His father told him, "Fear nothing, for Allah is inside your ribs and between your shoulder blades, like an armor." He never saw his dad after that morning. Nadim's father was diagnosed with lung cancer that fall and died 59 days later, on a Monday in March. Zahra heard that story many times.

Nadim used to tell her stories to help her go to sleep when she was in the hospital, during her long recovery from surgery, when the pain was too bad and the morphine wasn't working as well as it once did. Nadim talked more when he thought she was asleep; those were the best parts. Zahra learned to fall into a light sleep and float on clouds of stories. The worst part was when she woke up, startled by sharp cramps in her shrapnel-torn abdomen, and he was gone. She never asked him to sit next to her bed and tell her stories. She hated waking up and finding him gone; it was better not to start, because the end always left her lonely and achy, like withdrawal from a drug she never cared for in the first place.

"25, 26, same thing!" Nadim said, he was using his "pay attention" voice, which was a little louder and more enunciated. His eyes widened and his pupils enlarged.

Today, Zahra wanted their time together done. She wished it was Sunday so they could both hate Sundays. It was Friday afternoon. The volunteer lady in pink was now on the phone with the upstairs kitchen, counting soda cans, pudding cups, and chicken rice plates she needed sent to the café. The only things the café cooks ever made there were fries and hamburgers; the rest came from the main kitchen. The woman tapped her crooked finger with red nail polish on the table in front of her. Her voice resonated through the empty café.

"No, no, no, that is not what I said. I said twenty servings of today's special, *yalla*, *yalla*, send it quick," she ordered.

She seemed pleased with herself when she hung up. She looked at her reflection in the glass partition separating her from the hospital lobby and ran her fingers through her blond straw-like hair. Her face was wrinkled and dotted with an assortment of dark spots.

Zahra thought about Nadim coming back to the doctor's café after she was gone. She pictured him talking to Mrs. Nabila and drinking the same juice: *Balkis*, orange *mawardi*. What she has always known him to drink there.

"How are you doing with leaving the city?"

"*Mniha*," she said.

She was not good though, but she was not going to tell him about any of it. She never did before, and it was too late to start now. He was sending her to another continent, another culture, and the chances were they would never see each other again. How she was doing was her problem today. Just like it was before.

"*Mniha*? That's it? Are you worried about the bag on the way?"

Zahra squeezed her eyes hard and looked towards Mrs. Nabila to see if she heard him. She felt a flush fill her and spill over her face and chest. The woman at the counter seemed absorbed in her reflection; if she had heard Nadim, she didn't show any signs of understanding what he was talking about. Nadim felt her uneasiness. He got close to her and almost whispered.

"I mean, do you feel comfortable emptying the bag on the plane?"

Zahra looked away, her face ablaze.

He worried about her colostomy and acted like the bag was his fault. He frequently came to her with colostomy "success stories," something about someone with a colostomy who figured out one thing or the other about living a full happy life and "staying open to the possibilities." The only possibility she was interested in was getting rid of that colostomy and not, literally, smelling like crap. When Nadim started his colostomy "pep talk," she stayed quiet until he finished.

She wanted to hear about Hajji, Nadim's mother and Zahra's companion for the past few years. She wanted to hear about his job. More than anything she wanted him to tell her that he would miss her and wished she was not going.

"How is your mother?" Nadim asked.

"She acts all sad about my travel. She is convinced I will find a husband after I get my green card," Zahra said.

Nadim giggled, he was relaxed again. He could bring up her mother any day and they would chuckle.

Nadim started to dislike her mother soon after the accident. He was the only one in the hospital who saw right through her theatrics of love and devotion to her daughter. Zahra was simply a meal ticket to Fatima. Once Zahra's engagement to a wealthy man fell through because of the stigma of her injury, Fatima turned her wounded daughter into a second-best lottery ticket. Neighbors treated her like the mother of a martyr for years. After an entire year of recovery in a hospital bed, Zahra was ready to go home, but Fatima's one-bedroom apartment was too "inconvenient" according to Fatima. Fatima gave Nadim many reasons why Zahra couldn't get to her follow-up appointments in order to learn to live with her colostomy. Nadim, in frustration, suggested he might find Zahra a long-term care facility. He then asked Zahra if she would move in with Hajji, his mother, whose memory was failing and who could use someone like Zahra to keep her company. A few months into living with Hajji, Zahra realized that she was never moving back in with her mother. Fatima got rid of Zahra's pillow. The bed the two once shared had one pillow placed in the center.

Zahra's time with Hajji eventually turned into a job, the only job Zahra felt comfortable doing without feeling bad about her colostomy. Fatima acted surprised when Zahra informed her that she would continue to live with Hajji. She told her daughter that it was very difficult to live alone but that she would be willing to live alone so that Zahra can have a job and help with the "house."

"I left Lebanon for seven years, only came to visit once," Nadim said. She already knew that it was for his father's *talet*, the third day after his burial. He missed the burial. Muslims don't wait to bury the dead, not even for a faraway son.

"When I came back, it was the same country; different on the outside, same on the inside. I doubt people there ever change."

"You said you changed and that it was worth leaving for seven years." She was repeating his words to him, hoping he would start talking about himself and stop mentioning the bag.

"I did change. I was ready to change, to see what moved people, what colored their world, to be free and to meet myself.

22

You will meet a side of yourself, a side you didn't think existed Zahra. It will be worth it in the end."

Leaving the country was Nadim's idea. He had been talking about it for years, like an enchanted ride he wanted her to get on to get as far from her current life as possible.

Zahra resented herself for not being able to feel excited or happy about her immigration to America. It was as if she was in an empty room, waiting for someone to tell her what was next. She knew leaving Lebanon couldn't undo the last ten years of her life. Nothing could. The reason she agreed to leave was Nadim. For years, he talked about opportunity, about a world where people who were different were not shoved to the side like trash. Nadim cast this miraculous image before Zahra. All she saw was a mirage.

However, when the day finally came, Zahra didn't have it in her to let him down. America meant that she could come back changed someday, with stories and courage like his.

"Take care of Hajji and of yourself," she said.

Her throat was so tight that she didn't try to breathe deep. She collected her small bag from the chair next to her and was getting up. Nadim's pager had gone off a couple times; he had reached and pushed the button to stop the beeping without even looking at the screen. That always made Zahra nervous. He was a heart doctor, the kind that made a difference between life and death. Nadim always said he was a tool in God's hands. She had stopped believing in God before they met.

They shook hands, Nadim tried to get close to hug her, but she turned her face. He understood her body language and tapped her on the right shoulder instead.

"Be happy, Zahra, it's possible!" He handed her a paper bag and asked her to open it once she got to Kansas, and a book for the road—*The Unbearable Lightness of Being*, by Milan

Kundera. He spoke about this book many times, but she hadn't read it yet.

"I signed it for you," Nadim said. He giggled and she looked away.

This was not the time to give her his favorite book, as they were parting ways, possibly forever. She clutched the book tightly, put it in her backpack, and started to head out. That was how it felt to leave one's heart behind, Zahra thought.

Chapter Two

The air felt hotter after being in the café with air conditioning. The first moment of walking into it was the worst; heat carried people's misery much more efficiently than the artificial frostiness of Mrs. Nabila's empty diner. Beggars on the sidewalks of the hospital called, languorous and out of refrain.

"*Yalla ya helweh, alef, alef,*" a tiny, bronze-skinned girl called to Zahra.

The little girl was no taller than three feet. She had big green eyes and hair, sticky from henna, poking out of her little head in every direction. Zahra knew that beggar—she always hung around that corner, seemingly unsupervised. She usually asked for 500 liras or a sandwich. She wanted a thousand today.

Little beggar girl got a raise, Zahra thought as she shook her head "no" to the little girl and kept walking. The girl was too hot to follow her up the street into main traffic, like she had done on cooler days.

A few feet up the street was the van stop. This used to be the worst part about heading back home—the crowded sweaty van. Zahra could wait for hours at the intersection and unless she was willing to spend money for a full cab, a taxi, no car would take her back to Hara. Today was the last day the van ride would exasperate her, the last time she would hope the smelly men would keep to themselves, the last time she would be stuffed into a van with a broken door and more than ten passengers.

The next morning, her neighbor would be taking her to the airport. She told Nadim he couldn't, that was the only thing she asked him to do for her, let her figure out her airport ride. She touched her middle, over the oversized black T-shirt; a squishy bulge met her hand. Zahra felt her face get full of blood and her throat constricted again. The van seemed full, but the driver was still on the sidewalk hustling more passengers.

Greedy, slow driver, she thought. Zahra needed to be still, as any extra movement or extra emotion meant a likely leak under her shirt. She sat next to a woman with two toddlers and a baby and looked out the window. The woman shushed her screaming baby.

"*Yalla, yalla* mama, *kaman shuway*," the woman said in a Syrian accent.

Zahra wanted to tell the starving baby that his mother was lying, it was not *shuway*—there would be a lot of time before they got to where they needed to be. The baby seemed to read Zahra's mind and screamed louder. One passenger started to leave the van, told the driver he was not paying to go deaf. The driver surprisingly started driving with a wave—"go"—after the crabby customer barely gotten out of the door.

The music got loud, almost drowning the infant's wails, and there was finally some breeze coming through the window. Zahra looked out at the fancy stores lining Hamra Street, and she hoped people on the van stunk worse than her bag.

Hajji's face came to her mind. Every afternoon just about this time, Zahra used to cut up fruits in cubes and move Hajji

26

to the balcony of her fourth floor apartment. They would both sit away from the railing and watch the cars on the street, the pedestrians, and the shops underneath the building they faced.

There was a grocery store, which Zahra avoided like the plague. The man who ran it always insisted on asking Zahra a million questions about Hajji, he then proceeded to ask Zahra about herself, and finished his long monologue by telling Zahra that she is a fine woman and that Hajji is lucky and well-loved by Sayidna Mohamed for having such a caring and lovely nurse.

Zahra always felt the urge to correct the grocer that Mohamed couldn't logically love Hajji and allow her to completely lose her memory like she had, and that she was not a nurse. Zahra usually let him finish his tirade and eventually figured out how to avoid walking in front of his store. Instead, she walked around the block and down the street to another grocery store, a real supermarket. That supermarket had more expensive vegetables and fruits, but the price difference was well worth it, and nobody seemed to care about who Zahra was and where she worked.

Zahra thought about Hajji sitting on the balcony without her, with the new help. After Zahra's trip was finalized, Nadim hired a nurse from the Philippines to replace Zahra. Over the last week before Zahra finally moved out of Hajji's house in anticipation of her trip, she explained Hajji's routine to Connie, the nurse. Connie demanded to have the weekend off, but promised to find a friend of hers to stay with Hajji then.

Zahra felt something like worry infiltrate her mind and weigh her chest down. She knew that Hajji didn't know who was sitting next to her—lately, Hajji had stopped talking all together. Her emotions seemed as nonexistent as her words. Zahra continued to care for Hajji as if Hajji knew that the fruits were well-washed and all cut in the same size, that her blankets were always washed, and that her hair was combed and put up in a perfect gray bun. When Zahra brushed her hair, Hajji made faces similar to those a protesting toddler would make, but never pulled away or complained the way a toddler would. That face was the only expression that Hajji made lately, and it became what Zahra looked forward to in the morning.

Hajji spent her days looking at the soap operas on TV. Zahra made sure to find her new episodes since the satellite receiver had over nine soap channels. Zahra could smell Hajji's sweet soapy smell on her clothes, a week after being gone from that house. It made Zahra tear up every time she noticed it. She always squeezed her eyes tight until the tears passed and the only thing left was a dull ache in her chest, where her heart must be.

Two days after Zahra left, Nadim called to ask her if there was a special trick that she used to brush Hajji's hair. He told her that Hajji started to scream anytime Connie got close to her with a hairbrush. After two days of not being able to brush it, Connie asked Nadim to call a hairdresser to the house to cut Hajji's hair.

Chapter Three

She got off the van with everyone else. The entrance of Dahia was always very busy. It always made her think of Dante's Purgatory.

It was a shame, thought Zahra that another author, Palahniuk, didn't visit this place and ride an overcrowded van before he wrote his stories about hell. He could have been more literal—no need for similes here. Hell was a city where, no matter how hard men worked, they could still not afford to spare their children need. It was a city where many of those same men thought women had only three reasons to exist; to tempt them, to taunt them, and to submit to them. Hell was a city with two faces; one where broken, overfilled vans brought mothers who begged all day on the side, the other full of multimillion-dollar apartments. Hell was that those cities were both called Beirut, one for the rich and the other for the underprivileged.

She couldn't think of the name of Palahniuk's book. She kept trying to remember, it was a good distraction. She had a couple more streets to walk and then she would be home, one last afternoon and one last night for her in this city. Nadim gave her the book about Hell last fall. It was written in English. Nadim said she needed to read English books because that was all she was going to find in America.

Fatima, Zahra's mom, was home, having coffee with the neighbor Oum Raja. The two women were sitting across from each other on a straw rug, in line with the breeze from a fan. A brown wooden tray with coffee cups and a small silver carafe separated the two women.

"*Salam alikoum* Oum Raja, *Salam alikoum* Mama," Zahra said.

The two women nodded, and Zahra walked through the living area to the bedroom and shut the door. She grabbed the clear saline squirt bottle and the gauze, then put them back. She could empty the bag for now and wait until the neighbor left to change it. Zahra walked back through the area where the women were now absorbed in reading the coffee cups. The women didn't bother look up from the cups. There had to be a scandalous revelation in the coffee grinds, Zahra thought.

She entered the bathroom and carefully locked the door. Fatima had moved the chair out of the bathroom again. She sighed and kicked the bucket on the side. At least it was full so she could use it to flush the floor hole after emptying her bag.

The ileostomy bag was now poking out of her black T-shirt, like a kid's inflatable toy. She needed to do this an hour ago, but she was in the slow van that stopped everywhere on the way. Zahra squatted over the hole in the ground, as best as she could, she had her thighs spread out around the drain opening. She hated floor toilets; they were messy no matter how she squatted over them with a bag. After her surgery and rehab the nurses asked Fatima to install a regular toilet, to make it easy for Zahra to empty her bag without splashing and having to clean the whole bathroom. Fatima told them those toilets would be unsanitary; she was a woman who washed herself for prayer and needed to keep her *wudhu* intact from toilet seats.

Zahra always wondered why the Allah her mother worshipped was so harsh and inconsiderate of differences. Zahra thought that people made a god in their image, and went on forcing that god on everyone else.

The dark hole in the white ceramic on the floor always reminded her of Nietzsche, ever since she read his, "When you look long into an abyss, the abyss also looks into you." Nadim told her she would like the book. "Books are windows with excellent views," he said.

She was not going to be stuck in that house with no proper toilet; she was not going to let the abyss look into her. At Hajji's house, Zahra had her own bathroom; all her ostomy supplies were on a table. When she came to visit her mother every once in a while, Zahra appreciated how much easier it was to clean her bag at Hajji's.

Zahra rolled her T-shirt up and tucked it under her brassiere; her stomach was hollow with pink scars running across it in every direction, like the chart of a busy city. She looked at the distended bag, rolled the end, and opened it over the hole. She watched the green slime go down and turned her face away to escape the splutter that she could feel on her legs and feet.

"*Kis ikhtak*!" she cussed under her breath. She knew it was not the bag's fault, it still felt good to curse it, calling his sister a whore. Zahra tried to reach to the side to get water from bucket to rinse her bag before rolling it back closed. The bucket was too far for her to reach, she cussed the bucket and got up holding the end of the bag upwards to avoid splashing herself with green feces.

After she rinsed and closed her bag, Zahra splashed water into the toilet and around it to clean her mess. She then lifted one leg at a time and kept it above the white floor bowl as she

31

rinsed it, she needed soap, but this would do for now, she thought she could wipe her legs and feet some more once she got to the room. She just wanted to get out of that small, smelly bathroom, even though the stink was all hers.

She washed her hands at the fractured sink. Fatima never had any good soap. No matter how much money Zahra left to buy soap and detergent, Fatima insisted on buying the green cheap olive soap that was sold by the kilo.

One more day, Zahra thought, and walked out back into the area where the two women were consulting their coffee cups.

"Your mother has a fortune coming her way, a lot of money," Oum Raja said to Zahra. Fatima smiled smugly as if on her way to cash the fortune check.

"*Mabrouk,*" Zahra said, trying to make her congratulations sound as sincere as her sarcastic heart allowed her. She had congratulated her mother on many non-materializing coffee cup fortunes before. Those never quite actualized for Fatima, but still deserved felicitations for daring to appear in coffee grinds. It was better than green shit down the toilet.

"*Boukra habibti*, you are leaving?" Oum Raja asked.

"Eh, in the morning," Zahra said.

"Who is going to take care of the lady you helped for years? *Ya haram* she will miss you so much," Oum Raja exclaimed.

Zahra hated when people brought up Hajji, asking questions about a woman they didn't know, most likely with the only purpose of feeling pity for her. Zahra never talked about how she spent her days. Every couple of months, her mother showed up unannounced at Hajji's house, to make sure Zahra was there, working, doing what she said she was doing. When Zahra asked her mother why she was there, Fatima acted

32

all hurt and said her job was to protect Zahra and keep other people from taking advantage of her.

"She has her son," Zahra said. She looked at her mother, hoping Fatima would join the conversation, giving Zahra some space to leave. Fatima looked at Zahra, her eyes hungry for a more elaborate answer. The two sitting women were still quiet, like good pupils eager to hear a story.

Zahra felt her insides slosh; she had nothing to eat since she headed out in the morning.

"Her son will figure out someone to take care of her. He can move back with her if it's necessary," Zahra stated as she walked past the women to the kitchen.

"She helped them so much, it's a pity she left without remuneration, she loved that old woman so much, my daughter didn't care about the money," Fatima declared.

Zahra kicked the kitchen table and raised her fists up. Fatima was trying really hard to get her enraged by bringing money up.

Nadim was very generous with the money he paid Fatima. He refused to give her any money initially, and insisted on paying Zahra herself. One day, Zahra asked him to give Fatima the money, that it would make it easier for Zahra who had grown tired of Fatima's visits; if her mom had the money, hopefully then Fatima would lose her motivation to drop in on Zahra. She figured sending her wages in her place was a fair trade.

Sure enough, as soon as Nadim started sending money to Fatima, her visits lessened and eventually stopped. Nadim insisted on paying Zahra too, even though she was content living with Hajji and having her wages sent to her mother. Nadim would not have it, and he gave her the option to leave or to stay and accept the money. She accepted the pay and saved all of it, over the following nine years. She saved it for the surgery that would rid her of her colostomy and scars in America. The doctor she visited in Beirut told her that the bomb has caused Zahra to lose most of her colon and that the risk of closing the colostomy was not worth taking. Zahra did not believe that doctor, she would prove him wrong. With enough money, there would be a surgeon somewhere who could help her.

Chapter Four

Mustafa, Zahra's friend, beat the alarm clock. His three-knock tempo woke Zahra instead. She tiptoed around her mother's sleeping body on the floor in the living room. Zahra was still half-asleep when Mustafa started to drag the bag towards the door.

"It's still early," she whispered. Mustafa was halfway out the door with the luggage.

"Early birds get all the seed, girl!" Mustafa said. He winked at her and gestured at the sleeping Fatima.

He was wearing his tight jean pants, a red shirt, and his shiny black pointy shoes. Zahra smiled. She went to the bathroom, brushed her teeth, and put her long brown hair into her daily ponytail.

"Please! Please! For once put something on besides a baggy black T-shirt!" Mustafa cried. Zahra brought her index finger to her mouth gesturing him to shush. She put her shoes on and grabbed her bag of ostomy supplies.

"Go downstairs, I will be there in a minute. I have to wake her up," Zahra directed, she gestured towards the door and flapped her hands.

Mustafa put his hand on his hip, stuck his tongue out at her, then turned on his heels and walked out the door like a wind-up toy. Zahra slipped a white envelope under Fatima's pillow and looked at her mother for a while.

"Mama, *yalla baddi rouh*," Zahra uttered as she gently shook her mother's shoulder. Fatima snorted a sleeping breath and opened her eyes.

Zahra smiled at her. She loved her mother the most when she was asleep. That was when all she could see was Fatima's hardships and long journey. The old lady couldn't hurt her with her disappointment and harsh words. When she slept, Fatima's pain was her own to carry, none of it could spill into Zahra's soul.

"Zahra *Allah yehmiki*," Fatima mumbled. Zahra didn't need Fatima's god to protect her or do anything for her; the biggest favor he could do her was stay right there in that small stuffy house.

"Okay, Mama," she said. She kissed Fatima's forehead and squeezed her one last time before springing up on her feet, heading out the door, and shutting it behind her.

Mustafa was sitting in the driver's seat of his black Hyundai. He had the windows rolled down and the music blaring Rami Ayach's newest song. Zahra didn't care for the artist, but Mustafa, who was a huge fan, played that song for her and danced to it every time he came to visit lately. Zahra got in the car and turned down the music.

"*Yalla!*" Mustafa exclaimed. He had his arms over his head and was waving them to the tune.

"People are sleeping! You want them to shoot you?" Zahra asked. She pulled his arms down and put them on the steering wheel.

Mustafa started to wiggle his middle and shake his head, dancing as he started the car. He was as wound up as ever at four in the morning.

"Zahra, promise to find me a boyfriend who looks just like Rami Ayach," he pouted.

"Look at you at four in the morning, Mustafa!" Zahra teased.

She shook her head and couldn't hold back her smile. She was kidding with him—she knew he meant an American boyfriend. That was all he talked about, ever since she told him she was emigrating. "How in hell am I going to find you some guy and then convince him that a Lebanese boyfriend is just what he needs?!" Zahra used to tell Mustafa every time he asked her.

"You figure it out! Your problem!" Mustafa would respond, and they would both laugh. "Let those idiots here realize what they missed out on!" Mustafa would always conclude as he pointed to himself up and down with fluttering eyes.

His eyes were big and brown with long dark lashes. Mustafa always dressed nicely, fashionably, no matter how broke he was. His wavy hair was usually gelled to perfection and parted to the side. His high cheekbones and chiseled jawline drew attention to him anywhere they went.

"Can I have my face back?" Mustafa always said under his breath when people stared at him, although he knew that his good looks were his biggest asset.

Mustafa tried to style Zahra's hair, but she always put her hair up in a ponytail no matter how perfect he told her the cut was. Mustafa told Zahra that she was gorgeous, that her long thick hair was enviable, but she never saw beauty when she looked at her own face. It was a lot easier to see Mustafa's.

Mustafa came to visit Zahra every Thursday, his day off. Hajji seemed to like him. He danced for her and even got her to clap for him a few times. He always stayed with Zahra and Hajji for lunch, and left late in the afternoon.

"To do laundry, since my mom knows not to touch my clothes! Too delicate for Oum Issam's barbaric laundry ways," he pointed out.

Zahra met Mustafa when she was sixteen, before she got injured. Mustafa was the brother of Issam, a man Zahra was engaged to for a couple of days before the injury. Afterward, Issam's mother, Oum Issam deemed Zahra was not "suitable material" for a future daughter-in-law, and the engagement ended. That was the only good thing that came from her injury, Zahra thought.

Mustafa kept showing up at the hospital long after the rest of his family had stopped. Zahra didn't care for him at first, but Mustafa eventually grew on her. He became her best friend, the one who knew everything about her, not that there was much to know. He told Zahra all his secrets, his disappointments and victories.

Mustafa drove them out of the neighborhoods to Tarik el Matar, the airport road. The neighborhoods looked nicer, the buildings newer and taller the further they got away from Zahra's neighborhood. The sidewalks were wider and cleaner. Green-clad Sukleen workers were emptying trash dumpsters and sweeping the sides of the roads. Mustafa drove them by large billboards that advertised "diamonds to charm her heart" and "swimsuits everyone will envy." The women on the boards looked European, with little noses and blue eyes. The ads were for tourists and wealthy Lebanese people driving to and from the airport.

Mustafa hummed to the song the entire way. Zahra looked at the road and wondered if she would miss anything about it, about the buildings, the heat, and the blonds on the billboards.

The day was breaking over the mostly empty road. The cars driving by were either cabs or sleepy travelers going to the airport.

They pulled into the underground parking lot next to the elevators. Mustafa carried the luggage and Zahra walked behind him. The parking lot smelled like cigarette smoke, Mustafa coughed and fanned his face with his hand. Zahra had never been to the airport. In fact, she had not even seen most of Lebanon. After her accident, she mostly stayed with Hajji.

Nadim sometimes insisted on taking them either to have ice cream or go for a car ride. Hajji didn't do well with long trips; neither did Zahra's colostomy. Nadim told her that Wichita was flat, much bigger and more spacious than Beirut, and that it had no traffic. She tried to imagine Wichita, but she couldn't. She looked it up online and the pictures were just as foreign as her empty imagination for it.

"You packed all your black T-shirts and black sweatpants! I was hoping you would leave some for me to wear!" Mustafa joked.

He always picked on her clothes, his choice of color and style was as grand as his ego; having an "unstylish" friend, as he called her, affected his social image! Zahra often reminded him that the only society witnessing their friendship was Hajji, who didn't know black from blue.

Mustafa assured Zahra that he knew his way around airports. He explained the entire process to her about three times, until she begged him to stop repeating himself. Between Mustafa and Nadim, Zahra could get to Wichita in her dreams.

"Don't forget to look at the monitors and the signs, the toilets have a blue sign of a woman," Mustafa said. Zahra nodded. She could feel her bowels getting more active; anxiety always won when it competed with her guts.

"Mustafa, this is for you. It's for you to rent your salon. It will give you a start, you do the rest," Zahra pronounced and handed him a white envelope.

Mustafa started to cry. He shook his head "no" and kept crying as she kept pointing the envelope towards him.

"Mustafa, you will pay me back. You can't live forever talking about your salon—it's time." Mustafa was weeping silently, looking at his feet.

Zahra was not expecting this much sadness. Mustafa was dramatic but this was bordering tragic, worse than she had ever witnessed when her friend cried. When Mustafa dated Aziz, his married boss, for six months, then had his heart broken when he went after some other guy, Mustafa cried for days. A while later, he showed up all bubbly with a story of a new crush.

Mustafa's tears today seemed bitterer. He appeared increasingly upset as Zahra got closer to leaving. Zahra wondered if she should have left the money in the car, instead of having to witness Mustafa's tears so close to her departure.

"I have to go, I need to have plenty of time to change and clean my ostomy once more, this morning is making me nervous, you know how bad that is for me!" Zahra said, her voice teasing him, hoping to get her cheerful friend back.

Mustafa wiped his face and sniffed a couple times then grabbed Zahra's arm and walked with her to the Middle East Airlines counter. He had an ex-boyfriend who worked there. He told Zahra fifteen times how the guy had texted him to be sure he was coming with Zahra today.

They waited behind a couple of families with many suitcases. Mustafa jumped out of line and made a beeline to a bald guy in an airline uniform who came out of the back to help behind the counter. The father of the family in front of them began to protest. Mustafa swung around and assured him he was "not going to affect the rest of his life," and to "please relax, his friend needed extra assistance."

Everybody in line turned around and looked at Zahra, who glared at Mustafa. Mustafa was behind the counter now with a hand resting on the bald man's shoulder. Both men had wide grins and animated expressions as they talked for a bit. The airline guy nodded and occasionally erupted in loud chuckles to Mustafa's outburst of stories.

Mustafa grabbed Zahra's bag and snatched her passport from her hand with a wink as he handed it to the airline guy. The people in front of them were now being checked in by the other open employee and, instead of giving Zahra their hateful looks, they were arguing with the woman behind the counter about the extra weight of their bags. When Mustafa finished checking Zahra in, he returned, fanning white papers with the Middle East logo on them and pushed them in Zahra's direction.

"He upgraded you to business! Business *habibti*, that's the life!" Mustafa exclaimed.

Zahra took the papers and slapped him on the head with them. Mustafa ducked and chortled his effusive laughter. Mustafa waved to his friend behind the counter and then walked Zahra to the security checkpoint. As Zahra started heading towards the airport officer, Mustafa's tears returned.

"It's okay, Mustafa, I will call you when I get there," she crooned.

He nodded, pulled her toward him, and squeezed her for a long time. He was still sobbing when let her go.

Zahra was finally at the gate, bag cleaned, boarding passes in hand.

"Check monitor, follow signs, bathroom is outline of woman in blue," she repeated to herself.

It was time to board before too long. Zahra followed people into the line. A woman in red and navy scanned her boarding pass and Zahra walked into a long hallway with no windows that ended at the entrance of the plane. Another woman in uniform gestured Zahra to her seat. It was a blue padded chair with buttons on the side and a footrest in front of it. A dark-haired woman in red and navy blue came by Zahra and buckled her belt.

"Champagne, Madame?" the hostess asked.

Zahra shook her head no and looked out the window. Soon after the hostess went over safety instructions, the hostesses sat down for takeoff. Zahra felt her insides separate and her heart dig into her ribs when the airplane sped on the runway and lifted into the air. It wasn't until her head stopped sinking backwards into her chair that she dared to open her eyes. Her tongue was hurting—she had bitten it hard when the airplane aimed for the sky.

Outside the window, she saw white puffs above the sea. Zahra smiled at the blue Mediterranean underneath. Zahra avoided the sea ever since getting hurt by the bomb while she was swimming. Something about being so high above it made the sea seem tame, it sparkled in the sun like the back of a small snake. Zahra smiled at the blue and looked at the clouds. She was going to America, where, ironically, the bomb that ended the life she knew was born. She hoped it was also where she would become whole again.

Chapter Five

"*Welcome to Wichita Eisenhower Airport,*" the illuminated runway sign said. Zahra pulled out her note pad from her purse.

- *Mary Malone at airport*
- *Follow luggage claim sign*

This was the last thing written on her card. The past two airports were just what Nadim described: big and busy, hurried people going in all directions. Zahra had enough time to clean up, and attend to her bag.

She refused all the food that kept showing up in front of her, except for one roll of bread on the way from London to Chicago. By then she was dizzy and her hands were trembling.

Her wait in Chicago would be her longest, according to the cards Nadim wrote for her. Zahra followed people out of the airplane, past the sniffing dogs, past security into a huge room where Americans went one way and everyone with a visa went the other. Zahra's bowels got restless during the immigration line wait. She couldn't leave now—this was officially the beginning of her journey into this country.

Officer Johnson was the name of the man who helped her. He walked with Zahra from the booth to a back room where people who seemed to have more complex situations waited.

Before he left the booth to walk with her to the "interview room," Officer Johnson paged his supervisor to ask if it was okay for him to stay with Zahra until she cleared immigration. He was a short man with red hair and a red beard. There was a snake tattoo on his arm with *"don't tread on me"* inscribed underneath it.

Zahra couldn't understand all of his fast English. He said "refugee" many times, and "help you." He kept asking her to write down what she was saying because he couldn't understand her accent. Zahra couldn't understand his either but she didn't tell him that. Officer Johnson kept offering her cookies in a blue wrapper. He pointed to his mouth as if she didn't know how where food went.

"I know."

"Have one!" he said with a victorious smile.

She gestured to her shirt and drew an imaginary circle where her ostomy hid from the insistent man.

"Sugar is bad for me," Zahra explained.

"Ah," he said, letting his hands and smile drop. "I will find you something else."

"Thank you." Zahra smiled, and nodded.

After leaving the immigration office in Chicago with a bag full of crackers, cheese, and a bottle of water, Zahra waited at gate A27. She devoured the sack's contents. Officer Johnson was a kind man, but the other officers in the "immigration room" seemed more like jailers. Although she had never met a jailer, she saw them in Hajji's TV shows.

When the old, skinny black man pushed her wheelchair to A27, he said "final destination" and pointed to the sign that said *"Wichita 9:45."*

She gave the man two of the five-dollar bills Nadim had given her to "tip" people helping her at the airport. She had forgotten about the "tip" money until then.

"Thank you, miss!" He sighed, looked around, and pushed the wheelchair away from Zahra. He looked slower pushing the empty chair away from the gate and back into the whirlpool of hurried travelers.

Zahra's eyes were heavy at the Wichita gate. She felt her surroundings turn into a dark humming as she fell asleep. The gate agent tapped her shoulder when it was time to board to her final destination. Zahra forgot for a moment that she was at a gate in an airport, farther than she has ever been from everything she knew and remembered. The agent gently smiled and pointed to Zahra's boarding pass that had fallen into her lap.

"Wichita. It's time," the agent said.

Zahra followed the passengers and didn't try to fight the sleep that claimed her as soon as she buckled herself in the seat by the round window.

The thump of the airplane against the tarmac awakened Zahra. She looked out the window and saw a dark runway illuminated by yellow lights on each side. She was dreaming of being in Hajji's kitchen, cooking for both of them. Hajji didn't know what day of the week it was, what time of the year, or what year she was living in, but she knew when Zahra was cooking and when mealtime neared. Hajji stopped looking at the TV screen in front of her and turned her gaze toward the kitchen.

Zahra felt happiest at that time of the day. She looked forward to setting the table in the kitchen and calling Hajji to sit down for the meal. Hajji seemed to recognize Zahra then, not so much as herself but as someone who cared for her and she felt grateful for. Zahra hoped Connie remembered everything Zahra told her about mealtimes, bath time, and the rest of the routine that surrounded Hajji and kept her and Zahra content.

As the person sitting next to Zahra got up and left, she followed him out of the airplane. She knew America was her new reality, there was no going back. She followed the passengers to the baggage claim, her eyes still heavy and her mind still refusing to wake up. Somehow sleepwalking felt less scary to Zahra than being fully awake and completely on her own.

A big woman with blond hair below the luggage sign was holding a cardboard sign with "*ZAHRA*" written on it in a fluorescent pink. Zahra walked to her and pointed to herself. She was too tired for English. Her legs were shaking from exhaustion and her bag was bulging against her skin. She bit her lip hard to keep her tears inside. She missed Hajji, she missed Mustafa. She even missed her mother. Her heart felt void inside her sagging T-shirt.

"Hi, honey! I am Mary, Mary Malone. Welcome to America! Welcome to Wichita!" Mary was screaming in Zahra's face, gesturing around her and smiling like she had been waiting at this airport all her life for Zahra to show up.

"Hello." Zahra pointed to the bag on the belt and Mary jumped to grab it.

"Let's go, Zahra! I am parked really close! This airport is so small, you don't ever need to walk too far! You must be exhausted." Mary didn't stop talking, not even to breathe.

Zahra followed into the warm humid night. She closed her eyes and fell asleep soon after Mary started the car. When she woke up, the car was stopped, and two women were by the door staring at Zahra and whispering to each other. Mary carried Zahra's bag into the house.

"Sweetie, *ahlan*!" One of the women greeted Zahra, in Arabic. She had red hair and a pretty face. She gently touched Zahra's shoulder and gestured towards the house. Her Arabic sounded Egyptian.

Zahra wondered if she was dreaming. The pretty tan face with big eyes kept looking at her expectantly.

"Ana Noor," she said and extended her hand towards Zahra.

Mary pointed to the pretty girl with red hair and yelled, "Noor, this is Noor!"

The girl and Mary nodded and looked at Zahra expectantly. Zahra looked at Noor and smiled. The other woman in the house stood behind Noor with her hands on her large hips and watched the introductions; she seemed disappointed with Noor and Mary.

"Will you just let her come inside the house? I am sure she is exhausted," observed the large-hipped woman.

Noor looked towards the voice and rolled her eyes. Mary laughed.

"Hold your horses, Diane! Always on fire, aren't you?" Mary declared while she gently tugged on Zahra's arm. "Come on, come on," she said.

Zahra followed the three women into a small, one-story house that smelled musty, like summer clothes that had been packed and forgotten. There was a couch, a big chair with ripped fabric, and many other things that Zahra was too tired to look at. The light was yellow and dim. It came from a lamp that stood in the corner with a ripped shade. In the faint light on the low blue couch Zahra sat, and next to her stood Noor, who was still holding on to the luggage.

"Beth from our church will come take her to her first appointment tomorrow. She needs her medical clearance before anything else," Mary told Diane.

Mary left, and soon Diane did too. "It's almost midnight, girls, I will turn into a pumpkin if I don't go to bed right now!" Diane said, laughing and then coughing as she walked into the next room and closed the door.

"Cigarettes and pipes!" Noor said.

Zahra looked at the closed door as if the cigarettes and pipes were holding Diane hostage in an ongoing coughing spell in that room. She nodded to the tall woman with pretty dark eyes and long fire-red hair. Zahra had never met anyone with hair like Noor's, it reminded her of cartoon characters and dolls. Noor flipped her thick mane as she carried Zahra's luggage to the basement bedroom. She held on to Zahra's arm as they went down the narrow stairs.

The bedroom was smaller than any room Zahra had been in: two beds, a wall closet, and a vanity by a mirror filled it to the door. It was bright from a light fixture that hung from the ceiling. It smelled like fresh laundry, unlike the smoky, musty smell of the upstairs.

"I clean this room to its bones and keep a ton of deodorizing beads in it!" Noor explained in English. Zahra didn't know what "dee-o-dor-eye-zing beads" were, but she smiled and nodded to Noor.

On the other side of the stairs there was a bathroom. It was tiny as well, but clean and well-lit. Zahra washed herself up, put on a new bag, and hoped the old one wouldn't reek in the trash. She used the last trash bag she had with her to trap it in. She would ask for more trash bags tomorrow.

After she sponge-bathed her body, she changed into another black T-shirt and sweatpants. She smiled, thinking about what Mustafa would say if he saw her right now. Zahra could picture him rolling his eyes at her lack of style.

When Zahra walked back into the bedroom, Noor seemed asleep. She was under her covers all the way to the top of her red hair. Zahra's watch illuminated to 12:48 a.m. when she pushed on its little button. She got into her bed and turned off the lamp.

Chapter Six

Noor was fixing her hair in the mirror, running her fingers through her candy red locks and puffing her lips while tilting her head to one side then the other. Noor smiled more to her reflection in mirrors than she did to anyone else, especially Diane, who brought forth loud sighs and occasional door slamming from Noor.

Zahra couldn't understand all of Diane's English, it was faster than the CDs she used to learn the language and sounded different than the many English books she had read. Noor was very eager to translate and throw in free comments about what Diane was saying,

"I did not say that!" Diane would sometimes scream if Noor took too many sentences to interpret Diane's words.

"How do you know what I am telling her?" Noor quizzed.

"Because I can see her face!" Diane said.

Noor threw her hands up in the air in despair and walk away from the two of them, the obligatory door slam followed. Zahra and Diane would sit in the uncomfortable quiet. Sometimes Diane would get a notepad and write down her thoughts and Zahra would respond in English. That seemed to make Diane always nod her head.

Zahra was ready to find a job according to Diane.

"Ask Noor to take you with her, you can make some money helping her. I need to make a better rent off of you guys."

"In Ramadan, we will work together, I can't do then what I am doing now," Noor proclaimed when Zahra asked.

Noor left for her "job" at four in the afternoon on some days, and returned in the early hours of the morning. She worked from her room with the door closed the other days. Noor didn't talk about her job in front of the computer or outside the house. She sometimes smelled like beer and always got in bed and covered her head with her pink blanket.

Zahra pretended to sleep as Noor got in the shower and when she later crawled under the sheets of the creaking bed facing her. That was the first time in her life that Zahra anticipated Ramadan.

"I can't work from the house online during Ramadan, I will help you then. It's a month when Sayidna Mohammed, *aleh assalam*, said to do more charity, sometimes the best charity is towards those you love the most!" Noor told Zahra.

She seemed pleased with her charitable plans and with telling Zahra that she loved her enough to make her a charity for Ramadan. Zahra didn't respond. They both lived in a basement room fit for unlucky mice, and seemed equally deserving of the charity of any season. Zahra didn't know anyone else who spoke Arabic and, although she had read books and watched movies in English, she had never spoken English until she came to America.

"Ramadan will happen a week after you get to America!" Fatima told Zahra before she left.

Fatima sounded disappointed then. Her mother was more than capable of enjoying Ramadan without her. They didn't live together, and their only exchange was that of money, given by Zahra and received without gratitude from Fatima. Zahra always gave her mother Eid money when that holiday came at the end of Ramadan.

Zahra didn't want time off from caring for Hajji. Their time together had no seasons and no holidays, just the soaps on TV and the occasional visitor.

Nadim always came to visit his mother on Eid. He had the day off and always seemed in a good mood. He always gave Zahra Eid money and books. She was not going to think about Nadim and his books this Eid. Noor would be a good distraction with the grandiose plans she was promising Zahra. They were going to the mall with Noor's boyfriend, Hussein. Zahra had not met Hussein but heard of him on a daily basis in Noor's conversations. Zahra was not one to ask questions, especially about Hussein, who never called or showed up. Whatever the plan was, Zahra agreed that it would be a glorious Eid.

The week before Ramadan started, with Noor working from her room and Diane smoking in hers, Zahra spent her time with Beth.

"The refugee buddy," as Diane referred to Beth. Beth was a member and employee of First Baptist, the church that sponsored Zahra's emigration. Beth's job, as she explained it to Zahra, was to help her "navigate the system." Zahra was not exactly sure what the system was in her case and how she would navigate it, but she nodded to Beth.

"When it's all said and done, you will be able to find a job, go to the grocery store, and use the bus. Hopefully, you'll make new friends and find a new home along the way," Beth said, Zahra assented.

Beth's voice that grew louder the closer she was to Zahra. Beth's excitement seemed in tune with her increasingly louder voice but irrelevant to everything else. Staying quiet meant the "refugee buddy" would talk less. Zahra needed medical clearance, paperwork, and hopefully a job soon.

Beth drove a red Hyundai she named Jelly Belly. She talked about that car as one would of a child. During the first week of going to get her medical clearance and other appointments, Zahra learned daily facts about Jelly Belly. Zahra smiled and nodded in hopes of avoiding reruns of the same story—something Beth did when she had doubts about Zahra understanding something. Zahra could care less if they drove a pumpkin.

"Jelly Belly, like the candy, you know! The one good thing from a divorce! I never even came close to driving a new car!"

"Nice car," Zahra replied. Every time the subject of Jelly Belly came up and Beth looked at Zahra expecting a confirmation of the narrative.

"Someday you're gonna buy a car! That day is gonna be amazing! Especially if it's your first car! I mean this really to me feels like my first car! It is my car, I don't have to share it with some bossy A-hole—do you even know what an 'A-hole' means?"

Beth exploded in laughter. It didn't seem like she was laughing at Zahra, more like she wanted Zahra to get the joke and laugh along. Zahra smiled and nodded.

A car would be nice to get some day, she agreed with that more than she agreed with the rest of Beth's stories. It would be nice to buy a car and learn to drive it. Nadim took her driving a few times, he showed her how to drive his blue Mercedes. He never seemed worried about her driving it into a wall in the parking lot where he showed her how to drive.

"In small town America, everybody owns a car. You have to learn to drive," Nadim told her.

She got more nervous with every lesson, her colostomy acted out with the longer distances that Nadim was teaching her to drive. Zahra would end the lesson by asking to go back to Hajji's house to check on her, even when she knew that Hajji would be napping for another hour. After those days, when the topic of driving came up, Zahra looked away and stayed quiet until Nadim stopped asking when she would practice her driving lessons.

Beth looked like she could be in her fifties, although she never shared her age with Zahra. Her face was long and pale, her eyes an anemic shade of brown and her hair parted in the middle along a gray line that became darker as it got away from her scalp. She worked with First Baptist, driving refugees in Jelly Belly to their appointments, and showing them how to use the bus. Beth told Zahra that she loved her job, although it didn't pay like her previous one, which was selling phone accessories at the mall.

"First Baptist is my church and when my pastor asked, I knew The Lord was calling me for more than selling cell phone chargers!"

Zahra was not sure at first who Beth's "lord" was. She talked about her lord a lot. Beth had more stories about her lord than she did about Jelly Belly and her ex-husband combined. When Zahra asked Beth who the lord was, Beth smiled and took her hands in hers and started crying.

"I was hoping you would ask some day. I wasn't going to intrude, The Lord's ways are gentle and mysterious. He finds a way to your heart in the end. Come to church with me and you will understand more."

Zahra realized then that The Lord was another word for God and that Beth was hoping to share her religion with her all along every time she brought up what "The Lord" wanted Beth to do. Zahra had no intention of going to church, she told Beth that on Sundays she is expected to clean Diane's house and run errands with Noor.

"Would you go someday, just once to see what it is all about? It is an amazing experience," Beth promised.

Zahra had no intention of meeting Beth's god or any god. She felt like her own argument against God was better than people's argument for him. The only two people she ever shared that argument with were Nadim and Mustafa. Zahra's God used to be a figure of authority that helped here and there when begged fervently. She was sixteen when she fired him after being hit by that bomb during the Israel-Hezbollah war in the south of Lebanon. She still got flashbacks of the salty water she was swimming in and the warm sand the bomb threw her into. The other memories from her teenage life were gone.

She did give her God a few chances after the accident but nothing good ever happened no matter how much she asked for it. After the air raid, Zahra spent over a year in a hospital bed with her muscles cut by shrapnel, her bowels eviscerated by the blow. She had to learn to walk again at sixteen after being in bed and losing her muscle mass. The worst part of the bomb and of Zahra's God leaving, were the thick brown scars that covered her middle and the clear bag that filled with excrement several times a day. She was reminded every day by the sight and the smell of shit against her skin that she didn't get the privilege of a god like the others.

None of that was Beth's fault, though. Zahra was not going to tell Beth about it and so she kept nodding and agreeing to Beth's painful stories about the believers and nonbelievers. According to Beth, the world consisted of two kinds of people: believers like herself and nonbelievers. The former group had an obligation to share salvation with the latter.

"But a nonbeliever has to take that chance, grab the rope, so to speak," Beth proclaimed.

Zahra wondered if the only reason the church sponsored her as a refugee was to switch her nonbeliever status over. Zahra wondered what was different about First Baptist that its members cared about saving others. In Lebanon, Zahra had experienced religious people as not only not interested in sharing their certainty in heaven, but also glad to see the others not make the cut. There, the reward of zealous faith was as much the certainty of superiority as that of salvation. Zahra wondered if that was not a result of how much more populated Lebanon was. Maybe Americans like Beth had more space in heaven that made them more willing to invite others along. Perhaps there was a reward system for inviting a buddy along, Zahra thought.

"Let's show you how to order food at McDonald's," Beth yelled, full of excitement, almost more than the version she manifested with the "Lord" conversation.

Zahra had no money to spend at McDonald's, but she didn't want to be rude, she would order water and it would be free. She knew how to order food at McDonald's, but she didn't know what else to do with her time. Noor would be in the room, on her computer, working. Diane would be smoking in her room with the door closed. The little sitting space outside her bedroom downstairs was dark and smelled moldy. McDonald's sounded like the best option for her afternoon.

Beth ordered the usual number one combo: Big Mac, large fries, and a large Diet Coke. She would tell Zahra about how she was "watching it" and point to people around the place who "just ate like it was kingdom come." Zahra was not sure what a "kingdom coming" implied, but she worried the answer was in another church invitation, and so she didn't ask.

"Tell me about you! What was your life like? Isn't it so wonderful to be away from all of it?" Beth's voice was loud and her eyes were big again. She put a handful of yellow French fries in her mouth and held off chewing them until Zahra replied.

"Yes."

"What did you do? I mean what was it like? I was told you got hurt in the wars over there! That must have been so hard! I am going to pray for you!" When Beth said "you" to Zahra, it always sounded like "yooooo." With it came an outstretched palm, like the one people used to point to the winners of beauty pageants.

"I was expecting you to be wearing the *hageeb*! You know, the cover for the head! I was surprised when I saw you that you didn't cover your hair. Gorgeous black hair and such a beautiful face! You just need to get some fat on your bones! You skinny little thing!" Beth effused. Zahra figured that she meant *hijab* when she kept gesturing to Zahra's head and doing circles with her fingers around Zahra's face.

"No *hijab* for me," Zahra said.

Beth nodded and beamed as she took a big bite of her Big Mac. She seemed very pleased with Zahra's answer, she made a "thumbs-up" sign to Zahra and mumbled "good" through a mouth full of food. Zahra wondered in Beth's world if a *hijab* was a worse curse than cancer. She hoped that she wouldn't find out.

Chapter Seven

It was six o'clock by the time Beth dropped Zahra off at the house. There was no sign of Diane on the main level. Her car was in the driveway, so she had to be home. Zahra was feeling faint from hunger, she walked to the kitchen and pulled the bag of groceries she bought a few days back from the refrigerator.

Diane asked Zahra and Noor to keep their groceries in bags labeled with their names. She told then that she didn't have too many rules, but that nobody touching her food was one of them—not having visitors was another, and keeping their mess to a minimum the last.

Zahra took a slice of white bread out of the bag, some *Laughing Cow* cheese, and sat down by the small table in the corner to eat. She wished Noor would open the door to their room. Zahra needed to sleep. Nadim had warned her about jetlag, he said she would get very tired in the afternoon and wake up very early no matter how little she slept. Nadim gave her some Melatonin pills to take at bedtime that she left behind, somewhere in Hajji's medicine cabinet. She tried to remember where the pills were, not because it mattered, but somehow knowing they were in a dark cabinet on a shelf was comforting to Zahra.

The soft white bread tasted good in her mouth as it broke down to pieces and slid down her throat. Her mouth was still full of white bread when she leaned against the beige wall and closed her eyes. She saw the white pills in a clear bag on a brown shelf in a closed cabinet inside Hajji's quiet house. It was early in the morning. The sun was not up yet in Hajji 's world, on the other side of the ocean. Zahra heard the noises of the day disappear and felt a hypnotic dark take over her senses. In this half-sleep, Zahra walked into every room in Hajji's house. She looked at the furniture, the windows, heard the car honks on the street even smelled the red geranium in the pot on the window. Zahra turned into a ghost in her dream. She walked around the place that felt like home for the last nine years. *Did the apartment miss her?* she pondered.

Did the kitchen sink know someone else was washing dishes? Did the geranium wonder why she wasn't watering it? Inanimate objects had no souls, no opinions or words, but if they ever did come to life they did in cartoons, Zahra speculated what those things would say about Hajji's house with no Zahra.

She woke up to the footsteps of Diane walking out of her bedroom and into the kitchen. Zahra usually avoided sitting in the kitchen when Diane was home, it was an unspoken rule that Diane got the upstairs and Noor and Zahra stuck to the basement.

"Is your refugee buddy done helping you for the day?" Diane asked.

Zahra nodded as she got up to leave the small kitchen. Diane's kitchen matched the rest of her house in being poorly lit, cluttered, and painted a color as pale as Diane's skin. Diane had thick salt and pepper hair that she wore as short as a man's. She had big dark circles and bags under her eyes. Diane's teeth were a shade more yellow than her furniture and her mood was a continuation of the dying lawn leaning toward her front door.

Diane opened her refrigerator and got a bottle of wine, she poured the wine into a blue mug that she kept by the side of the sink. Diane closed her eyes and took a long sip from her mug. "So what do you think of this country?"

Zahra started to head towards the basement, hoping it would make Diane think she didn't hear her.

"I mean those people from the church, they seem like they mean well," Diane continued.

Zahra stopped and turned around. It was obvious that Diane was waiting for an answer.

"Yes, they are nice," Zahra said. She was not going to answer Diane the truth about what she thought about America. Zahra knew that it was hard to judge the entire country from what little she had seen and the few people she had met so far from Wichita. Diane set her wine mug down and looked at Zahra with widened incredulous eyes.

"Nice, huh?" Diane smirked.

Zahra could tell that she was already half lit. Diane's good mood rose as the night went on, usually in direct proportion with the amount she drank and pipes she smoked. By midnight, she was usually laughing loudly at some show on TV and talking to herself. Diane's laughter typically ended as irrationally as it started with total quiet.

"Black out," Noor once observed and pointed upstairs toward Diane's room.

"You are either lying to yourself or to me, young lady!" Diane said. Her eyes were clear despite her already drunk voice. Zahra looked away, the pain in Diane's soul was echoing in the dim kitchen.

"I always wonder what people really think of us Americans. The most powerful nation in the world, the giant that everybody sees from the corner of their eye, even if they are not looking." Diane looked around the room as if the walls usually responded to her tirades.

"Let me tell you a thing or two about America. You have not been here very long. You still have a hope of seeing through the fake props set up all around you!"

Zahra nodded.

"I worked at a factory that makes airplanes—twenty-five years I worked on an assembly line. That factory had good seasons and bad seasons. Sometimes we had a lot to work on, and others we didn't. I always counted on showing up to work and doing what I was expected to do. Now, 32 years of assembling airplanes is a lot of assembled airplanes! Probably the airplane that brought you here too!"

Diane was looking intently at Zahra's face for a confirmation of the story. Zahra nodded again. She had no idea if Diane worked on the airplane that brought her to Wichita, she wanted to ask Diane if she worked on any military airplanes, ones that America sold to Israel along with the bombs the airplanes dropped on people like Zahra. It was too late, and Zahra was too tired to ask that question, so she squinted her sleepy eyes in a hope to keep them open until Diane made her point.

"When I turned 50, guess what happened?" Diane asked. Zahra guessed Diane was probably fired for being a drunk when she turned 50, but something in Diane's voice made Zahra wonder if she didn't become a drunk after she was fired.

"They finish your job?" Zahra said.

"Damn straight! That is a good way to look at it! Finish my job is exactly what they did!" Diane laughed in an avalanche of hacking coughs. She slapped Zahra's shoulder in a "way to go" gesture.

Zahra smiled. She wished that she didn't have to hear the rest of the story but Diane had pulled up a chair and seemed like she was just getting started.

"Before I turned fifty, I hurt my back on the job. The doctor kept me out for three weeks and when I went back, I couldn't lift heavy, or push, and so I had to work a different job from the assembly line. They put me on inventory. I thought I was going to get better and get back to the line, but the company went through work jobs and they eliminated my position at inventory. I asked if I could go back to assembly, and they said I would have to apply to that position. I was not a candidate for that position because I was too old to apply for it! So there you go! That is America for you!"

Zahra didn't dare ask if Diane ever tried to find other jobs, jobs that she was qualified for. She smiled to Diane, and stayed quiet.

"You can work all your life, you can be the employee of the month once, twice, three damn times! It's going to come down to you or the money, and the money will always win! Every single time! This country is great because it's rich, and it's rich because people do NOT matter!" Diane emphasized "not" by pointing her finger in the air and waving it in a back-and-forth "no" in front of Zahra.

"We have a lot of things, objects we must have for holidays, vacations, births and deaths, most of those objects are made in China! China makes the plastic and we cover our lives with it, because it's pretty and fun! This country, Zahra, is about being happy and fun which looking at you kid, you can do a lot better at being both!" Diane laughed so hard she was wheezing.

Zahra didn't know if Diane's story was over. She had nothing to say about Diane telling her that she was neither pretty nor fun. After everything Diane just told her, Zahra felt a sadness for her—a concern for the following nights that Diane would not have anyone to talk to about America, because Zahra would be in the basement and, someday, out of this house.

"I am sorry that happened," Zahra said, as she kept walking toward the basement stairs.

If Noor was still in the room, Zahra was going to knock and ask to go to sleep. Soon, Diane would be laughing at her shows, and the next thing would be sunlight waking Zahra up.

Chapter Eight

"You are *not* a person!" Noor preached in Zahra's ear on the bus they were taking to their first job.

It was the first day of Ramadan. Noor woke up singing songs for Ramadan and Mohamed and clapping her hands. She seemed relieved to have a month where she had to worship and follow rules. Noor didn't wear her usual pink frosty lipstick. She explained to Zahra that makeup on the lips was *Haram* during Ramadan.

"I don't fast. I tried and it made me so sick so the doctors asked I to stop, but I am not a *kafira*, I still follow the rest of the rules," Noor said, looking at Zahra to reciprocate with the ways she avoids being a heathen.

Zahra had nothing to say, so she got ready and headed out the door.

"You can be a rag, you can be the purple lavender detergent." Noor pointed to the bottle of Fabuloso in the tote. She seemed confident nobody could understand her Arabic on the bus.

"If you can't see, if you can't smell, if you can't hear, then you can do this job. People leave messes behind, although I honestly think they carry their messes with them! Everywhere! I mean, how can you be so dirty for a week and then cleanup for one day?"

Zahra put her head down. She was hoping that Noor would stop her motivational rant. It was not helping. Besides, what if anyone understood Arabic on that bus besides the two of them?

"Just pretend you are not real, and *they* are not real. It's better if you are a thing cleaning things!" Noor probed Zahra's face for approval after she stopped talking.

Zahra kept looking at the bus floor until it came to a stop. Noor handed her the blue tote of cleaning supplies and dragged the vacuum cleaner behind her like a disobedient dog. Off the bus steps, the sidewalk met them with a hot sun that felt insolent and precocious for nine in the morning.

"The house is just down the sidewalk," directed Noor.

Zahra nodded and followed. Noor had told Zahra, the previous night, about the woman whose house they were going to clean. Zahra didn't want to know, but Noor gossiped away as if her life depended on it.

"This one is a Christian, Ramadan is not even something she knows about, but she is Syrian and she wants her own personal slaves! That is why you and me, friend, have a job today!" Noor was talking in front of the house's door.

Zahra gestured her to stop just before the door opened.

"*Di,* Zahra," Noor said, and pointed to Zahra.

The woman looked Zahra up and down and nodded before walking away to her kitchen.

"We will start, same as usual, just like last year!" Noor yelled over to the homeowner. The latter was on the phone.

"*Ijit el khadmi,*" she said to the phone.

Zahra felt her face burning and her middle cramp. She had just gotten called a maid. She looked at Noor to see if she was hurt too, but her friend was headed towards a closed door. Noor opened the door then slammed it shut and made a disgusted face.

"It's the first day of Ramadan! Let's start by cleaning the bedrooms, instead of dealing with the crusted urine and soap scum that had been waiting for me since the last time I cleaned this damn place." Noor was as loud talking about the filth in the house as the woman had been about saying that the maids had arrived. Noor didn't seem intimidated by the woman.

A gag rose in Zahra's throat, she looked around for something that would distract her away from the stink that stuck in her nose. Everything around was dirty, cluttered, unattended to.

She followed Noor to the next room. A green comforter with pink flowers was on one bed, a blue superman blanket on the other. Neither bed was made. She wondered if they lived like this until someone came to pick up their things and clean their toilets.

"Animals with housekeepers," she said to the toys thrown all over the pastel squares of the area rug.

In the kitchen she could hear Mira, the lady of this messy hole, talking to Noor. They seemed to know each other.

"The Mexicans and the Arabs work hard and fast and clean right with soap and water, that is! Not just some detergent sprayed and wiped off everything," Mira said.

Zahra hoped Noor was moving and not just standing there running her mouth. Zahra felt a hate for Mira that rose out of her feet to her head and made her face red and hot.

"So what did you girls do over the weekend?" Mira said.

She was now standing in the door of the room talking to Zahra. Her unexpected appearance startled Zahra, who was making one of the beds. She saw a self-pleased grin on Mira's face.

"Nothing!" Noor yelled from the kitchen.

Noor would later tell Zahra that they owed those women clean houses, not a report about their whereabouts.

"She has never met you, but she wants you to provide her with some gossip. We are not human to her, but our stories are worth being entertained with! You know what she will do with your answer? Call her friend back and tell her our business! Maybe if they cleaned their own houses, they would be less bored!"

Zahra didn't think about Mira's motivation to ask her questions, but she knew that she didn't like Mira, and had nothing to tell her no matter what the question was. Zahra nodded and no until Mira rolled her small eyes and left the room.

Her gray roots were covered today by a recent dye job, dull brown hair with useless blond highlights. She looked unhappy to Zahra.

Noor joined Zahra in the master bedroom after she finished cleaning the kitchen, which she called "greasy, grimy, and fit for pigs!"

Noor checked herself in the vanity mirror across the room and smiled to her reflection. Noor's hair was red and long like Ariel the mermaid, Noor's favorite princess. She kept a toy Ariel on her nightstand and had an Ariel pillow on her bed. Mira showed up in the door again.

Noor batted her lashes and pouted her lips, looked at Mira, and said, "Lots to do if you want us to clean the whole house."

"The basement is small, it shouldn't take too long. I left some shirts that need ironed by the ironing table, too," Mira said. She smiled from her beady eyes, turned around, and walked her thick hips away from the room before Noor had a chance to come up with something to say.

Noor moved quickly from one wall to the other, picking up things, folding, dusting until the room was ready for the "shark": Noor's favorite vacuum that she dragged with her onto the bus. She had bought the vacuum cleaner last Ramadan at an estate sale.

"One day I was cleaning in a really nice neighborhood, nothing like this house here! And the house next door was sold, not sure why, maybe the owners got divorced. That is something very common here!" Noor widened her eyes after her last sentence like one would after revealing a secret.

Zahra nodded.

"Estate sales are much nicer than a garage sales, you can find treasures that rich people are too spoiled to appreciate!" Noor got back to dusting. She smiled at the mental image of estate sales and treasures she was meant to find.

It was noon by the time the entire mess was picked up and cleaned in the other rooms. The bathroom door that was still closed haunted Zahra's stomach and throat. She grabbed the Fabuloso purple bottle and splashed the floors with the clear lavender soap and shut the door back as quickly as she opened it.

Lavender piss, she thought to herself, and knew this was the last frontier before Mira handed them their fifty dollars. Noor was finishing up with the ironing. She heard her ask Mira if there was anything else.

"Slap you, I am so going to slap you," Zahra said to an absent Noor. She hoped they would find better clients—cleaner houses—after this one.

"Three more weeks and Mira would have to iron her fat husband's shirts and wipe her little boy's piss off the toilet seats," Noor commented.

The cleaning was finally done.

They walked to the bus stop by Dillon's on 21st and Webb. Zahra was wearing Dollar Store flip-flops that whipped the sidewalk with every step she took. Her jeans were baggy and covered with a loose pink "Free Baptist" T-shirt that Beth gave her.

Noor was quite a bit taller than Zahra. As they walked past a reflecting window, she made Zahra look very small. Noor's face was beautiful but looked tired and flushed. The sun that was beating down worse than Mira's cleaning requests.

"28 more days and I get back to my job! I don't clean houses usually," Noor announced.

Zahra knew that. Noor announced it every ten minutes ever since she met her.

"Why can't you keep your job in Ramadan?" Zahra asked.

"*Haram*" and "no way" were all Noor replied.

Zahra wondered what "forbidden" thing she was referring to exactly with her "*haram.*" Maybe after the month of Ramadan, Noor would tell her.

The two girls were both quiet from hunger and exhaustion when the bus finally showed up. Neither one fasted in Ramadan, but Noor insisted that they turned down the water offered to them and tell people they couldn't drink it. On the bus, they finally cooled off while they headed back to the house. Noor pulled out a water bottle and offered it to Zahra. The water was warm and Zahra spit the sip she took into a tissue. Noor giggled and slapped Zahra on her shoulder.

Chapter Nine

Diane cared very little about how Zahra and Noor spent their days, as long as they seemed to be leaving the house to go to some sort of a moneymaking job. She did ask Noor once a day, at least, when they would be able to pay "proper rent."

Noor called Diane greedy and selfish when she was not around, Diane shared an equally unfavorable view of her tenant. The two women had brief and gruff exchanges that left Zahra feeling discomfited and a little sad. Most of the time two doors, at least, separated the two. Zahra was often outside both doors, sitting on the sofa in the basement or the chair in the kitchen, waiting for Noor to take them to a cleaning job or Beth to show up in Jelly Belly.

Most of Zahra's orientation to "the system" was done. Very little clarity came of it. Zahra blamed it on English slang that left her confused most of the time. Beth's devotion to talking about Jesus, McDonald's patrons, and her ex-husband didn't help either.

For a woman used to spending her days sitting in a half-lit room with a demented quiet elder, Zahra found Diane's home lonely and boring. She looked forward to scrubbing sinks and making beds. Anything was better than thinking about Hajji, Mustafa, and Nadim.

She imagined them going about their days: Hajji staring into her television, Mustafa cutting women's hair, and Nadim talking to his patients. Nothing around Zahra felt real, not even the scalding tea that burned her tongue. She was a ghost floating through the streets of a foreign town with foreign people speaking a foreign language. Nadim asked Zahra to get a cell phone and start texting him every day.

"Download the free app, I can send you WhatsApp texts," he had offered.

She didn't ask Beth to take her to the cell phone store. Zahra had money for a phone and money for a one-bedroom apartment, even money for a car but that was her surgery money. She kept her ten thousand dollars wrapped in a thin cotton cloth that she wore on herself, tied to her middle, above her hips and just below her colostomy bag. Her baggy black T-shirts hid the bag and the money well. Zahra had plastic wrap around the money to keep it from ever getting wet.

Noor had not given her any money from the first days of house cleaning, and Zahra was too embarrassed to ask. She figured that the money was going to Diane for the rent. Noor always paid for groceries and bus rides, she seemed to really care about Zahra. Without Noor, Zahra would be in no position to work, since her work permit had not been mailed to her yet.

"The Arab women are used to hiring Mexican workers and paying them cash, we will ask for cash and promise them better work," declared Noor.

She told Zahra that she knew exactly what would happen once they cleaned one house well, the remaining houses would follow. Noor had the house cleaning idea all figured out. She knew some of those women from Ramadan of the previous year.

The following two days were very similar to the first house they cleaned. The only difference was that the women they were cleaning for became nosier as the week went on. The conversations were mostly about the houses from the previous days: how much they got paid, how long they worked, anything special that the lady of the house was preparing for. Zahra kept to cleaning while Noor seemed endlessly entertained in making up stories about the previous days.

"So tidy, that Mira! I don't even know why she needs us! *Habibti,* don't get me wrong, I am very happy to have the job! Nothing better than cleaning except a nice generous boss to clean for!" Noor said.

She giggled and seemed so pleased with her story that Zahra wondered if Noor didn't believe her tales a little bit. Noor even turned jobs down as the week went on.

"We are booked for the next three weeks, *habibti* Sawsan, Zahra can help you after Eid but I have to go back to my modeling job!" Noor told someone on the phone.

Zahra was sitting on the bed across from Noor, reading *How to Succeed at Anything.* She found the book at the Salvation Army store on her way back from cleaning houses that day. Noor insisted they stop there one day after they had cleaned a house on the same block as the store. Zahra only found disgusting smells while Noor giggled and sang to herself as she dug in piles of things.

The books on the crooked bookshelf in the back of the store were tattered, faded, and irrelevant. She had change in her pocket today, and she felt sorry for the book that claimed such a delusional goal as success at everything. The book was marked for a dollar and then marked down to fifty cents. Noor was very pleased with herself when she saw Zahra at the cash register with the book in her hand. She winked at her across the store and nodded with approval.

That day at the thrift store, Noor found earrings, a sexy tank top, and high-heeled shoes in size eleven. Zahra was only interested in finding a good book, to read but the old books on the shelves all seemed boring. Zahra brought one book to America with her and she couldn't bear to start reading it. It was the book Nadim gave her the last time she saw him.

She promised herself that she would read that novel after her surgery. She would read it again on the airplane on her way back to Nadim without a colostomy bag. She would have fluent English and stories about Wichita. By then, Zahra figured, she would surely have found opportunity to go to college. She wanted to become someone who didn't hide in baggy T-shirts and cleaned houses or babysat people who lost their minds long before they met her.

"I told you we would be so busy we'll turn people down!" Noor said, after putting her phone down on her bed. "I told Sawsan you would help her! She heard about how good of a job we are doing!"

"You told her we were booked, Noor, we only have three houses to clean all week!" Zahra said.

"Oh, *habibti,* I know exactly what I said. You just watch me convince them that it's best to call and reserve us now! To get the big fish, Zahra, you have to use the small ones as bait."

Noor threw her hair back and puffed out her lips like a fish in front of her phone screen. A camera click sound followed and then Noor shook her head "no" vigorously and clicked another picture.

"You wonder why I take so many selfies! I know you do!" Noor giggled.

Zahra smiled to her and got back to the "success" book. It was now talking about how "everything that happens, does for a purpose and making that purpose your purpose is the way to ride the wave of success." Zahra found that as crazy as Noor, and the rest of her life. Clearly, the writer of this book was not injured when he was sixteen. He didn't spend any time wondering about the purpose of bombs and wars. He was probably American, Zahra thought, and his country made bombs and sold them while people like her spent their life hoping their colostomy bags didn't smell.

"Teach me what you learn from this book," Noor requested. She laughed and continued messing with her phone.

Zahra rolled her eyes and kept reading. She loved philosophy books because philosophers attempted to understand situations—not to tell everyone what to do. Jobran, Camus, and Nietzsche always helped Zahra forget about her discomfort, at least for a short time. She kept reading because the books brought temporary relief and that was better than none. The first book she read belonged to Nadim. She was in the hospital and he had been sitting next to her reading. When she woke up Nadim was gone, but Jobran was there. She asked the nurse to hand her the book and before nightfall she had finished it. That day was better than all the ones that preceded it. Zahra felt less pain and more hope than she had in a while. After the Jobran book, she asked Nadim to bring her another one, and she never stopped reading since.

Zahra hoped Noor would take her to a decent bookstore and Zahra could buy a good book. Reading the silly faded book about success made her miss good stories—stories that didn't explain the world in simple terms of never and always.

Loud music coming from Noor's phone startled Zahra. She looked up and Noor was making dance poses in front of the mirror and laughing with every pose.

Noor ran across the small room and grabbed *How to Succeed at Everything* out of Zahra's hands and threw it across the room. It landed open by the pink bedspread, where it looked even more grotesque than on the shelf amongst the beat-up romance books.

Noor pulled Zahra toward the mirror, while still dancing. Zahra resisted some then let herself get pulled upright. Noor's big hands had shiny red polish on the nails and felt as strong as a man's grip. She shook Zahra like a doll in rhythm with the music.

"We nadi al saidi, wil shabab elborsaidi!"

The song called Egyptians from all cities and towns to vote and Noor shook her head and clapped her hands to the rhythm of the drum, the guitar, and the backup singers.

"Hey! Hey! Hey! Hey! Hey!" Noor clapped, shook her middle, and arched her back, then moved back and forth in a circle with her serpentine body. She lifted her chest upright and threw her arms in the air and waved them side-to-side to the rhythm of the song. Noor threw Zahra a kiss and a wink as she flipped her hair.

Their reflections on the old mirror made Zahra feel like a sandcastle hit by a wave. A salty cold swell hit her heart out of nowhere and her chest shook in sobs. The song talked about Egypt finding her voice and hope for her people.

Something about the thin voice of the man and Noor's dance and her hopeful eyes broke Zahra's heart. In the mirror, Noor still danced. Zahra stood still. It took a few seconds before Noor realized that Zahra was crying. She stopped dancing mid-movement and grabbed Zahra in a big hug.

Zahra let herself sink into her friend's strong, wide shoulders and rest against her chest. She heard her own sobs like one hears a stranger crying. Zahra was shaking against Noor's embrace. The tears spilled from of her eyes, despite Zahra fighting them.

Noor let go of Zahra to grab the phone and turn off the song. She held Zahra again in the now quiet room. The silence made the tears sound and feel more real. Noor stood there embracing her and patting her on the back every once in a while, like one would a baby in a tantrum. The tears stopped after some time.

Noor gently moved Zahra away from her embrace to look at her face, as if to verify that the storm had passed. She took a corner of her nightgown and wiped Zahra's face, while still holding Zahra's hand with her other hand.

Zahra looked at her own fee. Mustafa would tell her that her toenails needed a pedicure if he saw them. He would tell her "*shou hayda!*" exclaiming at the state of her "*ijren shattafeh*" feet of a maid. She was a maid and her feet looked like those of one.

Mustafa would have grabbed some lotion and nail polish and changed the situation right away.

The two women sat on the bed, quiet and sad. Noor didn't ask and Zahra didn't tell her how much she missed home, or about how she felt completely lost in a land that had heat, dust, and strangers for miles on end.

"Tomorrow, we have no houses to clean, and I will take you to the cinema. It will be a great day!" Noor said.

Chapter Ten

Beth showed up at seven thirty to take Zahra to her Social Security appointment. It was Thursday morning. Zahra and Noor had a house to clean at nine that day—the mansion of a rich widow, according to Noor. Noor seemed right about her strategy to attract more business. After the day off Noor made them take, calls seemed steady and Noor was even able to choose which customers were higher paying and easier to work for.

Noor attributed the good luck that befell them to how much Allah and His Prophet Mohamed loved her. She told Zahra it was the reward Noor got from heaven for taking such good care of a friend during the Holy Month. Zahra was amused by Noor's convictions, although she did appreciate Noor taking her to the movies that week and paying for everything, including the soda that Noor allowed them to drink in public despite it being Ramadan.

"I don't know if she will be done in time for your morning appointment," Beth said, her voice high and curt.

"She has to be done on time, I am going to wait for her," said Noor.

Noor had opened the door before Zahra got a chance to it. Noor with her long hair and her morning-pale pretty face sprung out of bed towards the upstairs beating Zahra to the door. Zahra grabbed the folder Beth gave her a week ago to keep important papers in and headed up the stairs.

When Zahra got to the door, Noor was leaning in it with her arms crossed over her full chest that showed through a pink tank top. She sported baggy pajama bottoms with prints of colorful butterflies. Zahra walked by Noor through the door and Beth followed her down the narrow driveway.

"Bye, Noor, *shoofik bad shouway*," Zahra said, without looking at Noor.

She hoped it was true, that she would see her soon. Zahra didn't want to think about making Noor late to clean the dream mansion. Besides, the faster Beth took her to the Social Security office, the sooner it would be over with.

Noor disliked Beth as much as she loved being right. Her opinion about Beth was established, just like her opinions about other people. Earlier that morning, Noor went into a tirade about Beth's "bad" intentions for Zahra.

"Beth wants to convert you to Jesus. They worship Jesus instead of God! You are a goat—one they think is lost and needs help. Didn't she already tell you about Jesus waiting for the goat to return?"

"She has not said anything about me being a goat," Zahra replied.

"Maybe it's a sheep or a lamb, something like that," Noor offered.

"She didn't say anything about a sheep or a lamb either. Her job is to get me all those papers, and hopefully she will help us get customers from her church, like she said."

Zahra did remember the invitation to meet Beth's Lord, but didn't feel like watching Noor get more self-righteous that morning. Besides, Noor was just as convinced about her way to a god as Beth. Zahra could care less about either god. The mention of any god, any religion, left her with a sick feeling and thoughts she was sure not to share with anyone except Nadim, who was smart enough to know better but still chose to believe against logic and common sense.

He told Zahra that he felt God like someone feels a cold breeze on a hot day. Zahra told him that her days were all hot and no breeze. To Zahra, life was governed by random laws and stupid regulations. The world convinced her a little more every day that there was nobody behind the absent order.

Beth seemed relieved once Zahra walked out the door. They got into Jelly Belly and drove away. Noor still stood in the door. Zahra stuck her head out of the window and took a deep breath.

It was going to be another hot day. The small lawns along the block were mostly dried up and yellow. Some houses had kids' toys scattered in front of them, but no kids playing. In the nicer neighborhoods, the ones where Zahra and Noor cleaned houses, the lawns were green, the cars were parked in garages, and kids' toys were neatly put away in bins, never in front of the houses. The morning humidity reminded her of Beirut, she closed her eyes and pretended she was in a cab, on her way to see Nadim at his clinic. He always insisted on buying her lunch, and she always insisted on not eating it. She took it home and ate the food with Hajji in the dim living room in front of the soap operas on TV.

"Your friend Noor is not very happy today," Beth commented. It sounded like "Nooo" when Beth said "Noor."

"She is worried about being late to the cleaning job," Zahra alleged. "We are trying to get more houses."

"Her dressing like a stripper is not going to help! Her red hair won't either! If she looked like you, Zahra, people would want to hire her. I don't have a husband at home and I still

79

would not hire her. Honestly I don't like you living there. I hope that situation changes for you someday."

Zahra nodded, and kept looking out of the window. She felt her cheeks flush in displeasure, but didn't say anything to Beth.

Noor was a good friend, the only friend she had away from home and the only one she could speak to in Arabic. Zahra got tired of having to think before every sentence after hours of speaking English to Beth. The longer the day had been, the harder it was for Zahra to find the right words in a language that she had only heard on TV shows with Arabic subtitles that clearly translated whatever was happening on the screen.

Noor had lived in America since she was fifteen. She told Zahra that they moved after her father won the "Green Card Lottery." Noor seemed to enjoy being in America. She loved visiting Egypt but was always gladder to return home. Zahra wondered if America would ever feel like home, if having two homes was possible, unlike having two hearts.

Noor stopped wearing her tight tank tops and short skirts on the first day of Ramadan, she told Zahra that no matter how indecent a person was, she got a chance for forgiveness during the Holy Month as long as she followed the rules.

"People have to want help to get help. The Lord says ask and you shall receive!" Beth was still going on about Noor.

Noor had applied to be a receptionist at Green Meadows landscaping company. The owner was a member of First Baptist who wanted to help Noor. However, Noor ended up leaving the job a week later. In Noor's version of the story, the boss asked Noor to change the way she dressed and to stay off her cellphone. She told Zahra that she didn't enjoy the job and made more money modeling online.

"*Mosh liyya*," she told Zahra, who could see indeed how that job was not for Noor.

The Social Security office had a line of people that extended all the way to the sidewalk. People were waiting before the doors even opened. Zahra was more worried that she wouldn't make it to the nine o'clock job on time. She imagined Noor pacing the living room while Diane smoked in the kitchen. Beth got in line behind an elderly man who was speaking to his daughter in Spanish.

It didn't take long for the doors to open and people to enter the room. Everyone took numbers from a machine that beeped and spit a new number every time someone pulled a stub from it. The walls were a dull beige color, one that matched the expression of people sitting on the gray metal chairs. Zahra sat on a chair next to Beth who pulled out a book with a black cover and BIBLE written on it from her bag. Inside her book were highlighter marks of previously read passages, yellow and pink fluorescent lines ran across the pages. Beth didn't tell Zahra her usual stories, instead she kept reading in her book until Zahra's name was called.

The two women walked up to the window where Beth asked Zahra for her passport and refugee documents and handed them to a woman behind a desk, with "*Officer Gerald*" written on a small white sign on the table. Beth became animated telling the woman behind the counter about Zahra's journey as a refugee, something about war, about being injured and in the hospital. Zahra smiled and nodded every time the woman looked at her in disbelief. The officer shook her head in dismay at Beth's stories and eventually was just nodding. Beth kept talking and the woman filled out a form on a computer screen in front of her.

"Alright darling, you should receive your Social Security card between two and four weeks. It will come in the mail to the address on your immigration forms. There is a one-eight-hundred number on this form, you got questions, you call it."

"Thank you," Zahra said and followed Beth back to the car.

It was ten past nine on the wall clock at the Social Security office when they left. Zahra felt sad for Noor, she hoped she left without her.

Beth seemed in no hurry to get Zahra back to the house.

"Would you like to join the young singles group at my church? Lots of great friendships there, I hate to see you so alone."

"Yes, thank you."

Zahra hoped Beth would forget or an excuse would come up. She hoped some cleaning jobs would come up that would spare her from the young singles at Beth's church.

Noor was jumping up and down in the driveway when she saw Zahra in the red car from a distance. Noor was wearing skinny blue jeans and a purple T-shirt, loose enough to keep Beth's comments at bay. Once they got to the driveway, Noor ran to Beth's window and asked her to give them a ride.

"If you drop us, we can still make it on time, you made her late, don't make her lose her work for the day!" Noor said, her words were as agitated as her gesturing hands.

"If you ask me nicely, I will take you, I would do it, so Zahra won't have to work on Sunday," Beth declared.

"Noor, *Khalas*!" Zahra said, asking her friend to stop being rude to Beth.

"Okay, please! Please! Please?" Noor said with an affected smile.

Beth gestured to Noor to get in the car and in a second Noor was in the back seat with her vacuum cleaner and basket of cleaning supplies. She clapped her hands like a kid.

Jelly Belly stopped in front of a green lawn with colorful flowers and a huge house. It was nicer than any house Zahra had seen even in movies.

"Fancy!" exclaimed Beth.

"My friend is the hairdresser of the lady who lives here, he fixes her hair every day, EVERY DAY! She has a full-time housekeeper who lives here but she is on vacation in a Mexican country. It's possible that housekeeper will come back and not find her job!" Noor pronounced, pleased with herself.

Chapter Eleven

A slender old woman with silver hair, a slightly hunched back, and olive skin opened the door.

"Hello, Mrs. Jeha, I am Noor, and this is my friend Zahra."

The woman studied Noor and Zahra for a moment, then without a word gestured them inside her house, her thin forearm heavy with a multitude of diamond bangles.

Zahra was trying hard not to gawk at the spacious living room she could see through the atrium. Silky Persian rugs covered some of the shiny marble floors. From the ceiling over her head hung a chandelier with sparkling crystals dangling a stretched arm away. There were paintings on the walls of belly dancers and hookah smoking men wearing traditional embroidered outfits. The biggest painting seemed made of gold and precious gemstones that displayed a crucified Jesus. It sat on a mantle under a spotlight that made the colors shine even brighter.

The house did not look in need of any cleaning. Zahra had never seen a cleaner house in her life. Furniture, light fixtures, and area rugs seemed part of a grand plan of extravagance and perfect order. Zahra felt a ball in her throat; she was scared to move in that house, let alone clean it.

She thought about Mustafa, how he would be jumping up and down and flapping his hands in excitement if he stood here with her. Mustafa used to show Zahra and Hajji Television shows about mansions in Hollywood. Neither Zahra nor Hajji ever cared about the mansions, but Mustafa went on and on, comparing out loud the celebrity homes to his disinterested audience. Here she was, standing in one of those homes, wishing it was Mustafa instead of her getting intimidated by all that wealth.

Noor cleared her throat and put the vacuum cleaner next to the entrance door, as if it was not invited to the event.

"You can leave it outside, I have one that is gentle with the rugs."

Noor laughed nervously. Zahra saw fear in Noor's face, and it suddenly made her realize how much she cared about her friend. Her own fear gone, she walked to the door, opened it, put the vacuum cleaner outside, then closed the door gently. The woman gestured towards the cleaning supplies in the basket carried by Noor and Zahra took the basket from Noor and set it outside the door next to the vacuum. She locked the door this time and walked past the atrium into what looked like a dining room to the right.

"All the cleaning supplies are inside the utility room, I need you two to clean all the windows, dust, vacuum the floors, then use the special marble detergent to mop the main level." Noor and Zahra shook their heads in unison and walked toward the utility room as if hit by the same spell that made the rest of the house obey Mrs. Jeha's requests. The only exception to the gray woman's order was the crucified Jesus above the mantle, who seemed too preoccupied with what the men in the picture were doing to him to mind the stern homeowner.

The work requested by Mrs. Jeha took most of the day. By the early afternoon, Zahra felt dizzy and hungry. The glass vases, porcelain eggs, and bronze statues she was dusting felt

85

like an endless punishment. Noor swept, vacuumed and mopped. They tackled the windows together.

Noor and Zahra were carefully putting up the cleaning supplies, brooms, mops, and vacuum back in the closet when Mrs. Jeha reappeared with her stone face and wiry manicured fingers holding cash. Without a word, she extended the money towards Noor, the way one feeds an animal across a wire fence.

"Thank you very much! We can come back anytime you need us! Just call me!" Noor said.

Her voice was shaking again. The woman walked towards the door and Noor followed her. There was an awkward silence that ended when Zahra and Noor were reunited with the vacuum cleaner that waited for them outside the door like a good friend.

"Let's stop at McDonalds and eat everything they have! I am starving, *rah moot*!" Noor threatened that she was dying but her voice was happier than it had sounded all day.

She flipped her long wavy red hair and pulled the vacuum cleaner behind her, filling the fancy neighborhood with heel clacking and vacuum clunking against the sidewalk.

"Tomorrow, we go clean Mrs. Jeha's daughter's apartment. Apparently the daughter doesn't even live there but the apartment needs cleaned! That's the thing about rich people, Zahra, they are wasteful enough to give the poor a bite, but never a bite big enough to fill you up."

"So in your story, I am the poor?"

"You and me both, girl! We are salt beggars! Without salt you die, yet to get it you must die! A slow death shining clean windows!" Noor laughed and swung her plastic basket back and forth. The detergent spray bottles shook in sync with Noor's colorful silver bangles.

Chapter Twelve

The apartment they went to clean on Friday was vacant as Noor promised the previous day. The concierge opened the door and gave Noor his number to call when she was done cleaning so he can lock up after them. Noor batted her eyes and flipped her hair and giggled the entire five minutes the man was letting them in. When he left, she winked at Zahra and gestured towards the door he just exited.

"He likes me! *And* I have his number now! Did you see how he gave me his number! He wanted me to have his number!" Noor seemed convinced of the story she was telling.

The man seemed pretty serious, and quite old for Noor. Zahra was relieved that it was the concierge and not Mrs. Jeha letting them into her daughter's apartment. That woman made Zahra's insides freeze, the mere promise of not facing her stern eyes again put Zahra in a good mood.

"This is the nicest apartment building in Wichita!" Noor exclaimed. "Unlike Beirut and Cairo, where people live in apartments, here most people live in houses, the exception is the young and the poor. But not this apartment, this is a luxury building, people pay cash for those big apartments. It is a prestige thing!" Noor was on a roll, she talked fast and gestured to the windows and the rest of the apartment.

"In this building you can't rent, people pay in cash for the apartments, in cash, and it's not cheap! It's mostly retired people, high security for the old people who lose their minds, like your boss in Beirut!" Noor said.

She laughed as she gestured to her head and made a circle sign with her right hand by her ear. Zahra giggled and started to dust the large room with leather sofas and wooden shelves. There were long windows that showed the city as far as the eyes could see. Downtown was on the far right with its buildings. Zahra recognized some of the buildings she went to for her immigration papers.

In the middle of the large living room stood a glass statue that looked like a tree with colorful shapes sticking from its sides.

"A five-year-old can make better art!" Noor gestured towards the statue and paintings hung on walls around them.

"You want to know why nobody lives here, don't you?" Noor asked.

"No, not really."

"Of course you do! You are curious! Everybody is!"

"I am curious to know how many times we will clean this clean, vacant apartment before she realizes that she doesn't need us," said Zahra.

"Zahra *habibti*, you clearly don't get it! They need us to clean so they can be assured that their things are nice, that their houses are pretty. They don't look at their things, they don't use their space. If they did, we wouldn't really be here! Having maids is one of the things that remind them of their wealth!"

On the shelves there were framed pictures, one of Mrs. Jeha and a man who could have been the deceased husband, another picture showed Mrs. Jeha and three women. They had her thin hair, small eyes, large noses, and thick brows.

"Equally unattractive and sad looking," Noor pointed to the picture.

"Those are her daughters. No sons. Shame. Sami told me that she wanted a son but couldn't have one. She was always very jealous of women with sons. Sami, my friend, her hairdresser, says she is disappointed with her daughters."

Noor picked up the photo frame with the mother and three daughters and was pointing to it. Zahra felt bad talking about the people who were paying them for not one but two places to clean. She hoped that staying quiet would make Noor stop her gossip rant.

"The girl who owns this place! She never had to work a day in her life! She starts those business endeavors that always flop. Now her lover in Beirut is the latest and greatest adventure."

"Good for her! She can afford to lose money," Zahra said. She looked around at the quiet space as if Mrs. Jeha was hiding in a closet ready to confront both of them for gossiping about her daughter.

"Sami told me that the daughter is in Beirut because the man is trying to run away from her. He does not want her! But she wants him and so she just moved over there! She is sponsoring his project! He is building apartments with her money!"

"Noor! What they do with their money is none of our business!"

"Do you blame him?! If I looked like her, I would have to buy love too!" Noor said.

"Can you play us some Nancy Ajram, Noor, *dakhilik*, please?!"

Zahra loved when the music played and they quietly cleaned. She would even settle for Noor playing her music in her headphones and leaving her alone. She wanted to finish this place and go to the store. Noor promised they would take a different route home and stop by Wal-Mart, where Zahra could buy a phone. She missed Mustafa and Nadim. They had both called Mary twice since Zahra got to Wichita. Mary was the contact person for Zahra when she first arrived to Wichita, even though she had never seen her again since Mary gave her a ride from the airport. Mary, like Beth belonged to "First Baptist." She saw Beth on Sundays and that is how the message on a small piece of paper got to Zahra.

Two men called, each twice to check on Zahara, their names are Mufasa and Nadi. Read the message.

Beth was very curious to find out about who those men were. When Zahra said "friends," Beth raised her eyebrows and smiled more than usual.

"Maybe it's time you call them, it looks like they are really worried about you," Beth said.

Zahra would text them today after she got her own phone. Noor seemed to be certain that it could be done. Zahra moved fast. The songs on Noor's phone made both women move a little faster. Noor stopped every once in a while to lift her arms up and move them together in rhythm with the music. She waved her waist, threw her hips from side to side while shaking her chest and clapping her hands. Zahra laughed and went on cleaning. The place was cleaned in less than four hours; they opened every kitchen cabinet, emptied it, cleaned it, and then put the contents back, as Mrs. Jeha had instructed them to do. She wanted the apartment "deep cleaned."

"Call your boyfriend! You have his number! Let's go!" Zahra said.

Noor laughed and slapped Zahra's shoulder.

"Not my boyfriend! I only have one boyfriend! Hussein, *habibi*! The man I will marry some day! This guy is good for fun though! Maybe he can even get us some more apartments in this building to clean! Maybe another apartment nobody lives in, just like this one!"

"Okay, just call the concierge and let's go!" Zahra said.

She heard Noor talk about her imaginary Hussein before, the knight in armor who would show up any minute to sweep her into an enchanted life. Zahra figured that one of those days Hussein would either show up or Noor would stop talking about him.

The concierge named Anthony showed up as soon as Noor hung up, he must have been really close. He seemed a little nervous around Noor, who used her soft bedroom voice with him.

"You can text me if someone needs us to work for them, or if you miss me!" Noor said to a red-faced Anthony.

He mumbled something as he opened the lobby door and got back inside slamming a big glass door behind him.

The July sun replaced Noor's good mood minutes after walking in the midday heat towards the bus stop. Both girls were quiet as they sat on the bench waiting for the bus.

Chapter Thirteen

The following week was busy for Noor and Zahra; they spent hours on the bus to get to houses. Jobs seemed to be on opposite sides of town, and bus stops seemed miles away from the houses they needed to get to. They arrived flushed, sweaty, and tired before even beginning on the hours of endless cleaning requests.

Noor promised Zahra customers like Mrs. Jeha with clean, empty houses, and some of the houses were fancy and clean, but most were the cluttered and messy homes of women who always bargained more work for no extra pay from Noor and Zahra. The housewives hovered over their heads and wanted one more thing done, just as Noor and Zahra thought they were finished.

In the evenings Noor's good spirits always returned to her and she had scandalous details to relate about some conversation she overheard the housewife of the day relate on the phone.

"You know this last one we cleaned for? Her sister is getting an abortion! I heard her talking about it. She said "*rawhi, rawhi*," what else would she be wanting her sister to lose?" Noor's excitement was barely contained by her loud whispers.

"I am sure their church doesn't agree about killing babies. No church does! This woman sits on the board of the Christian school she sends her kids to. I bet she doesn't approve of abortion there!" Noor was still going about the presumed abortion story.

Zahra felt bad for people's lives becoming tales that Noor told, however Zahra never said a word to stop her. Zahra figured that was Noor's logic for making the work they did more bearable. For Zahra, the thought of saving enough money to change her life got her through many soiled floors and smelly bathrooms.

Diane was in the living room watching her shows on TV as Noor and Zahra made themselves dinner sandwiches in the kitchen a couple feet away.

"Maybe she wanted her sister to get rid of a cat!" Zahra said.

She took a bite of her labneh and olives on rolled pita bread and swallowed the orange juice that Noor poured both of them in red plastic cups. Diane didn't like dishes in her sink, and Noor's solution was to buy disposable plates and cups to end the sink conflict.

"It was a pregnancy—her sister is not even married! That is church-going people for you. The religion of good appearances!" Noor said. She whispered loud enough to be heard from across the street.

Every time Zahra answered, Noor put her finger to her mouth gesturing her to be quiet. Noor's scandalous stories seemed equally distributed between people of different religions and religious practices.

"Nothing like a Muslim married to a Muslim whose kids insist on eating ham sandwiches! Tstttt!" Noor exclaimed this one day after she found ham while she was cleaning the fridge of a Muslim family.

She carried the plastic package of ham into the bedroom where Zahra was cleaning the floors, and shook it in front of her like a dead animal. Noor prided herself on not eating pork. She warned Zahra against eating pepperoni on her pizza, telling her it was a pork derivative and that she hated to see Zahra unintentionally offend Allah.

Zahra was a lot less interested in the stories than she was in making money and adding it to her money pouch that she always carried tied to her waist. To Zahra, customers were people she would forget as soon as she left. Just like Noor advised her a long time ago, they stopped being people when she started cleaning their messes.

Zahra wished Noor followed her own advice, yet knew better not to tell Noor anything. The only thing that usually came from opposing Noor's opinions was making those opinions firmer than ever. Nodding was easier than listening to a lecture.

By the third week of Ramadan, Zahra was losing hope of ever saving money from cleaning houses. The rent to Diane, food, and transportations was using up most of the money she made. Zahra still did not have a phone. Without enough credit history, her application did not go through. She waited with Noor by the booth where a man wearing a blue vest helped her fill an application for a phone, and then apologized to her because the application was not accepted.

"You can buy a prepaid phone with prepaid minutes, miss," the man said.

"No, she doesn't need to waste her money like that!" Noor answered.

94

She grabbed Zahra's arm as she pulled her away towards the women's clothing aisle. Noor loved Wal-Mart. She showed Zahra the nice colorful underwear section and told her that once Ramadan was finished, she would be back to buy herself some nice lingerie to model in. Zahra nodded and smiled, but she was sad about the news she just got about her poor credit. That day Wal-Mart was no longer the busy place full of every single thing anyone could possible need. It became a reminder that she was still a ways from being like the people shopping down the aisles.

As she walked outside with Noor, she asked her more about the credit history predicament.

"You get good credit paying credit card bills and rent. The rent you pay here doesn't count because Diane doesn't have a company, she rents under the table."

"You can pay me cash and use my phone," Noor said.

Zahra decided to wait until she had enough credit for a phone to call Nadim and Mustafa. They would find out that she was safe and busy with her new job if they called Mary's phone, since Beth updated Mary about Zahra's progress every Sunday at church.

That day Zahra promised herself that she would apply for a job at Wal-Mart. There were employees in blue vests speaking English worse than hers, and who seemed successful at what they were doing. She hoped that she didn't need good credit to apply for a job at Wal-Mart, but she was not going to ask Noor that day.

Once Ramadan was over, she would fill out a job application, without telling a soul about it. She couldn't see herself cleaning houses much longer, even if it paid twice as much. As much as Zahra resented America for providing the Israeli bomb that made her life impossible, she knew that the only way to get her life back was in America. It would start with a good job, then good credit, and the rest would follow.

Chapter Fourteen

Beth showed up in the evening. She asked to speak to Zahra about some First Baptist families who had housekeeping jobs for her.

"Just you, Zahra, they don't want more than one person at a time working in their house."

Noor stood in the door with her hand on her hip and the other one in the air waving in front of Beth. "If you think you can separate us, you don't even know how wrong you are! I am the one who found all the houses we have cleaned so far!"

"I understand, but she is new to this country and needs all the help she can get!"

Beth's voice was shaking; she sounded like a kid pushing back tears.

Beth was always dressed in a pair of jeans with an elastic waist and a "First Baptist" T-shirt. She had those T-shirts in all the colors and each had a different verse printed on it. *"Be still and know that I AM GOD"* was the one she wore that evening.

Zahra felt really bad for Beth, she hated not being able to invite her inside the house. Having visitors was against Diane's rules. Zahra knew that Diane would be out of her room if the argument starting between Beth and Noor didn't end very soon.

"Thank you, Beth, maybe you can give me the numbers on a paper and Noor and I can talk about it."

"I have one family that's expecting you tomorrow, I can come get you at eight in the morning. It's my friend Sandy, I told her all about you, your experience with war."

Beth talked about Zahra's life before moving to Wichita to anyone who would stop and listen. Zahra was often standing right next to her as Beth described with a voice fit for a TV narrator the hardships survived by Zahra. She had never told Beth much about surviving anything but somehow Beth imagined a story where Zahra barely escapes death and then survives with awful pain and gets saved by First Baptist Church, particularly the prayers sent by members that result in her safely arriving in "her new life" in Beth's words. Zahra wondered if making up a horror story that ended with her being saved wasn't part of the "job description" of being sponsored by the church. That was why she never stopped Beth or corrected her; the truth was somewhere in the middle with parts worse than Beth could imagine and the parts of it better than the life in Wichita.

"Maybe you can tell your friend Sandy to find someone else, we are very busy tomorrow!" Noor said, before Beth finished her sentence.

Zahra pinched Noor's arm "*Khalas* Noor, *bass*!" She urged her friend to stop but Noor was getting louder by the minute.

"Is this your way of thanking me for being a good friend for Zahra, the only friend she really has! If she shares my business then it's fair I share hers! Isn't fairness and good what you guys are all about?"

Beth looked away from both of the girls and towards her car, as if the answer was inside Jelly Belly. Zahra got between

Noor and Beth, pushed Noor inside the house, and shut the door. She was standing in the dark humid heat with Beth who was tearful.

"I would help Noor, she needs a lot of help, but I am afraid she will get fired again," Beth stated.

"Please give us one chance. I think if you help her one more time, things will change for her," Zahra pleaded.

She was trying for her own sake as much as Noor's. She hated cleaning houses and Noor's presence with her was the only thing that made it bearable. Noor was the only proof she had on long days of endless window cleaning that Zahra was not just a maid, someone who shows up to clean other people's messes. Noor always knew what was behind the fancy doors and elegant dresses, she saw and heard through the nice things they owned and artificial lives they inhabited.

"Alright. Tomorrow morning, I will come pick you guys up at eight. Make sure she dresses appropriately," Beth said to Zahra, while pointing at Noor.

"Thank you so much, we will be ready! Noor doesn't wear short dresses in Ramadan, you don't have to worry."

Beth looked confused, but too much in a hurry to understand what Zahra just said. She got in Jelly Belly and waved Zahra goodbye.

Zahra stood for a moment watching Beth drive away down the block, her lights reflected on neighbor's houses before disappearing into the night. Zahra sat down on the concrete in front of the door and took a deep breath with her eyes closed.

She imagined Beth and Noor getting along and the next day's job being easy and paying well. The humidity was making her colostomy bag sticky and itchy; she looked up to the sky and saw stars just like the ones she used to see as a little girl.

"Counting the stars gives you *talool*," her older sisters warned her. She started avoiding looking at the stars all together; the last thing she wanted was a wart on her fingers.

She wondered if Americans discouraged counting stars too. She would ask Beth sometime if they were around stars again.

Chapter Fifteen

Noor didn't go with Zahra the next morning. She told Zahra that staying home and not making money was better than listening to Beth on the way to and from the house. Zahra didn't try to convince her friend otherwise, and went upstairs to meet Beth.

"The house is small and there is not much mess to clean up, but get to know those people, you could babysit for them someday," Beth said. She seemed sincere about wanting to help Zahra find a steady, reliable income.

When they rang the doorbell a very pregnant blonde woman opened the door. She had a pretty face and tired blue eyes. Her hair was back in a ponytail and she panted as she spoke.

"You must be Zaheera, I am Sandy, and it's so nice to meet you! I've heard so much about you!" Sandy grabbed Zahra and hugged her.

Zahra was pressed against Sandy's hard protruding abdomen before Zahra had a chance to realize what was happening. When Sandy let go of Zahra, she had an expectant look on her face, but Zahra wasn't sure what to say so she said nothing. Zahra looked at Beth, who stood right next to them smiling.

Beth pointed to two blond children who were standing close to their mother inspecting Zahra with curious looks.

"This little boy is Jeremiah and this little girl is Moriah. Guys, this is Zahra, my friend!" Beth said.

"I am not a little girl! I am Moriah!" the girl screamed. She kicked the floor and got closer to her mother.

"Yes! I forgot! Silly me! That's Moriah, and she is a big girl!" Beth said.

She extended her arms to the blond toddler who hid behind her mother. The little boy quickly lost interest in Zahra and went back to a pile of building blocks. Sandy gestured Zahra into the kitchen right next to the small living area.

"It's not much house, but it's our home," Sandy stated. Zahra nodded, she just wanted to know what needed done to get started.

Beth excused herself and left. She told Zahra she would come back to pick her up by noon.

"Please vacuum the floors then mop the kitchen." Sandy pointed to a vacuum and a mop. She smiled the whole time she spoke to Zahra, in a slow loud voice, like the tone one would use with someone who didn't speak the same language.

"Okay—no problem," responded Zahra.

Zahra got busy and hoped Sandy would stay out of her way. It was a good thing Noor didn't come with her—she would have been rude to Sandy. People like Sandy always brought up Noor's cranky side.

"Mommy, why is she here?" One of Sandy's kids kept yelling and standing in the way of Zahra's mop.

"Jeremiah! Inside voice, please! She is here to help Mommy, now I need you to stay out of the vacuum's way and let her do her job."

"But I want to help you, Mommy!" the kid screamed and kicked.

Sandy got on her knees and whispered into his ears something that made him get back to his building blocks in the family room. Before too long however, the little boy was back in Zahra's way. She didn't look at him, ignored his presence, and moved the vacuum out of his way, Sandy reappeared in the room and grabbed the boy by the hand and dragged him out kicking and screaming.

"Time out for somebody who is being very bad!" Sandy said, and the boy's screams turned to sobs that went on for a few more minutes.

The girl had golden hair and a smile sweet like her mother's. She stood on one side of the room and stared at Zahra. The girl ran to the next room every time she looked up from the vacuum. When she turned off the vacuum, Zahra heard the girl talking to her mother in the next room.

"Mommy, why is she touching our things?" queried Moriah.

"Because she was not born in this county, sweetie, and something very bad happened to her, and now our church is trying to help her become American like you and me. Jesus wants you to help thy neighbor, remember?"

"She is our neighbor? Does she have a daughter? Can I go play with her daughter, Mommy?"

"No, sweetie, she is our neighbor in Christ."

"Christ is our neighbor? I want to see baby Jesus!"

"Baby Jesus is in heaven, remember?"

The little girl lost interest in Zahra once she figured out that there was no play date or baby Jesus involved. She went outside and spent the rest of the morning playing in an inflatable three-ring plastic pool full of water. Occasionally, she would add tree leaves and toys to the pool. The little boy eventually followed his sister.

Zahra moved as quickly as she could, the carpet smelled like old cheese and diapers, she vacuumed it twice, but it looked just as brown and sticky as it did before she started. The furniture was not difficult to dust. Sandy's bedroom was full of baby equipment. She had a crib by her bed and a baby swing just a few feet away from it, by the window there was a changing table and a basket with neatly folded baby clothes. The two older kids shared the only other bedroom in the house. That one had two neatly made-up small beds and toys put away in a corner. Zahra swept the kitchen floor after she wiped down the cabinets and the table and chairs. She went outside looking for Sandy once she was done to let her know to call Beth.

"I am finished, unless there is something else you need me to do."

"Oh, thank you!" Sandy said, in her startled loud voice again. "Beth said you might be joining our congregation. We have prayed for you when you were on your way. I am so glad to see you here finally and safe." Sandy gave Zahra another tight hug, Sandy's belly pushed against Zahra's colostomy, more full as the day went on. Zahra pushed Sandy away gently and nodded.

"Thank you for everything," Zahra said.

Sandy called Beth and related to her Zahra was ready for her ride. She talked to Beth for a long time about Zahra and her good work. She looked at Zahra and lifted her eyebrows in a big smile after every sentence. Zahra was sitting on the sofa by the door. She didn't want to empty her bag in the one little bathroom that was just a few feet away from the living room. Zahra looked around at the house, it seemed even smaller than Diane's place and it didn't even seem to have a basement.

Facing Zahra was a bookshelf with pictures of Sandy's kids. The pictures were inside assorted frames. There was a photo of a smiling Sandy wearing a wedding dress. A man in a military uniform had his arm wrapped around her. Sandy still had that same cheerful expression, but her eyes seemed more tired and sad. Above the frame the quote said, "Therefore what God has joined together, let no man separate; Mark 10:9."

Zahra wondered who "Mark" was and how he spoke with such certainty about God. She hoped Sandy and her husband would not be separated, especially now that she had another kid on the way. Noor had told Zahra so many stories about married men who wined and dined her, promised her money, cars, and everything else she might need. According to Noor, most married American men cheat on their wives.

"But you cannot trust American men Zahra." Noor would intone. "They lie. The only man I would EVER marry is Hussein!"

Zahra hoped that would be the case for Noor. She hated to talk about men and marriage. Her dream life was one with no colostomy to manage, and Nadim close by. She didn't need to marry him, neither one of them was the marrying kind, but she could see them watching out for each other until their last day. Zahra didn't tell Noor that she owed her life to Nadim, and that he was the only reason she wanted to stay alive. It was too complicated of a situation to explain.

"You like the pictures?" Sandy interrupted Noor's thoughts. "Want to see their baby albums? My kids looked exactly the same when they were newborns!"

"No, thank you," Zahra said.

"I am so sorry, you must be exhausted."

"No it's okay, I am just ready to go home," Zahra declared. She hoped Beth would show up quickly to take her home.

Sandy looked hurt, she got up and left the living room. A few minutes later, Sandy reappeared from the kitchen with two twenty-dollar bills and a glass of juice. She handed Zahra the money and told her she was looking forward to seeing her in the young adult church group on Sunday. Sandy then handed Zahra the glass of orange juice.

"No, thank you. I am good," Zahra said.

"Please." Sandy insisted. "It's homemade. I made it just for you. It will get you your energy back." Sandy planted herself in front of Zahra's face and handed her the glass. Zahra took the glass, sipped and handed it back to Sandy who wouldn't take the glass from her.

"It's for you! Drink it all!"

Zahra drank the juice because she didn't know what else to do with a Sandy planted in front of her gesturing for Zahra to drink. She sat on the sofa feeling her guts grumble on the sugary liquid she just sent its way. She saw Jelly Belly pull up to the driveway and Beth stepped out of it. She got up and walked to the door, she felt nauseous and achy. The little girl ran to the door and stopped short of opening it after she heard the doorbell. She was in her purple and silver bathing suit and her pink plastic sandals. Sandy nodded to the girl's looks and the little girl screamed "yay" as she opened the door.

"Well, look who it is! Is this Moriah-the-big-girl's house?" Beth said. She bent and picked up the little girl, who held on to Beth's neck.

"This girl is baby Jesus's neighbor!" Moriah said and pointed to Zahra.

"Moriah!" screamed Sandy, with a flushed face.

"That's Zahra! She is my friend," Beth's voice was small and musical in echo of the little girl's tone.

"She will be saved! Jesus will save her!" The little girl looked at Zahra in hopes of confirmation.

Zahra walked up to the door, she was hoping nobody could smell the bag that felt very full and was leaking on her skin. As soon as Zahra heard the beep noise signaling the car's door unlocking, she opened the door and sat down in the passenger seat, sweating as Beth continued her conversation with Sandy in the driveway.

Beth drove carefully and always kept her eyes on the road. It looked like she was talking to her steering wheel anytime she talked to someone in the car.

"Soooooo?"

"They are nice people."

"Moriah is so funny. Such a smart four-year-old! She just had a birthday; I got her those sandals she was wearing."

"Nice," Zahra said. She took a deep breath and closed her eyes, looking at the road was making her more nauseous. She thought about her plane ride, how she stayed calm and didn't get into too much of a mess. She could do it again.

When Beth stopped in front of Diane's car, she wanted to talk about the coming Sunday, but Zahra felt a warm liquid touch her hands through the T-shirt. She ran out of the car and into the basement without being able to say another word to Beth. She felt sour juice in her mouth before she could get to the sink.

She barely made it to the sink, but she had still splashed on her shirt. Zahra closed the toilet and sat on it. She smelled of vomit and stools. The colostomy bag had leaked onto the money pouch she carried around her hips.

Zahra took the pouch off. The plastic wrap covering the hundred dollar bills was soaked. She wiped it down with a towel then got the money out. Only one bill was soiled. Zahra washed it and set it by the sink mirror. She took her clothes and her colostomy bag off and got in the shower. She stood under running hot water for a long time, crying and scrubbing her skin clean.

Chapter Sixteen

Zahra stayed in bed the next day, she told Noor that she was sick and couldn't get on the bus in the heat. There were five days left in Ramadan, then Eid followed. She would call Beirut from Noor's phone and wish her mother Eid Mubarak. Zahra also planned on sending Mustafa and Nadim texts to let them know she was doing well and working on getting her own cell phone.

Noor blamed Beth for Zahra's sickness, she was skeptical about Beth's friend as well.

"The only reason they help you is to turn you into one of them!" Noor said.

Zahra felt tired and defeated. She couldn't care less about Beth and Sandy's motives.

"You will lose your place in heaven! The only way is our *Nabi* Mohammed *Aleh Salam*!" Noor threatened.

Zahra didn't worry about going to heaven as much as she wanted to get out of hell. She nodded at Noor's self-pleased smiles. Noor made Zahra some tea that she set by her bed then left for her cleaning job of the day.

Noor was gone all day. It was the day to clean Mrs. Jeha's pristine house, particularly a pristine nursery that Mrs. Jeha had added to her mansion for the grandbaby that she was expecting any day now from China.

Noor went on and on about Mrs. Jeha buying a Chinese baby for her daughter so the daughter would come back and live with her. Supposedly, the daughter who left her mother's side to be with her lover in Lebanon wanted to have a child but couldn't conceive, so she decided to adopt. She didn't want to adopt any kind of baby though, according to Noor—Mrs. Jeha's daughter was only interested in a Chinese baby.

"I know you think one cannot buy babies, but I have news for you. You can buy a baby from any country and bring it here if you have enough money. That woman tried to buy a Chinese baby before for her daughter here in America, but the Chinese people took her money and kept the baby when she was born. Now, this time, she had someone go get the baby from China just so her spoiled ugly daughter can finally get her Chinese baby. As if there is a shortage of babies that need homes here!" Noor alleged—she seemed upset about this baby business.

Zahra wondered why Noor cared and how she knew so many details about people's lives. She knew better than to ask Noor, because she had tried to reason with Noor and her big stories before and got nowhere. Noor resented so many people for so many things; religious people were too strict and the liberal ones were too loose. She was glad that Noor seemed to love her and didn't try to change her too much.

Zahra stared at the yellow walls for hours. She looked at the book Nadim gave her, but didn't have the heart to open it. It was not time yet. Noor's bed had a hot pink cover on it, she had a nightstand with a blue lamp with star cutouts on the shade. When the lamp was on, Noor's stars projected on the walls.

Zahra kept the star lamp on all day. She spent hours looking at the ceiling and wondering what Hajji was doing at that moment. Lying in bed and staring around reminded her of the old woman who spent the past nine years of her life sitting and looking at whatever was in front of her.

Zahra never asked Nadim questions about what was going on with Hajji. The little he told her was the little she knew. He said that Hajji had a stroke, after which she was never the same. Nadim told Zahra that Hajji was not weak, but didn't know to move unless someone moved her. She could see and hear but didn't understand words the way people without a stroke could. Over the nine years that Zahra cared for Hajji, she became familiar with what Hajji needed and wanted. Words were not necessary between them. Zahra heard Hajji's requests louder than she would have her words. She figured out that if she listened to the silence in the dim room, she could figure out exactly what Hajji was saying. It was hunger, thirst, fatigue, and sometimes boredom. A simple language for their simple existence.

Back home, when Zahra went to visit her mother, Nadim cared for Hajji, Zahra would return to find him frustrated about Hajji. The old woman turned her face when Nadim tried to feed her. Even though he adored his mother, Nadim did not speak her language. Leaving Hajji was hard, but staying next to her was getting harder as the years went on.

When Nadim told Zahra about the opportunity to immigrate to America, the first thing that came to Zahra's mind was whether she could bear to leave Hajji. Nadim had spoken in front of Hajji about the travel, although Zahra wished he hadn't.

That night, when Zahra put Hajji in bed, she noticed that the old lady was crying quietly. Zahra held her hand and cried with her that night. The next morning, they went back to their routine, both pretending that they would have one another in that quiet house forever.

When Zahra woke up later that afternoon, Noor was sitting at the foot of her bed quietly texting on her cell phone. Zahra saw the cell light reflecting on Noor's face. She was sobbing quietly. Her mascara was smeared around her eyes. She looked beautiful even when she cried. Zahra had never seen her friend look so sad.

"Hussein, *ha yitgawiz*!" Noor said.

It was the first time Noor looked so broken, and so weak. Zahra got up and went to her friend. She held Noor tight while her friend shook and whimpered like a wounded animal.

Zahra wished Mustafa were here to help say the right words. She didn't know what to tell Noor about Hussein getting married, how to make it less painful. She stayed quiet, hoping Noor would tell her more about what was going on, how she found out. She hoped that Hussein was not serious about marrying someone else, but she worried that it would make it worse if she told Noor, so she stayed silent and held Noor in the dark quiet room.

"How long have you loved him?" Zahra finally asked.

"A really long time. He is the reason I wanted to have my surgery to become a real woman!" Noor said crying. She was looking at Zahra's confused face with a contrite expression.

Zahra understood at once why Noor was tall and had big hands, why she seemed to have men's shoulders and strength, and why she never undressed in front of Zahra even though she didn't have a colostomy bag to hide.

In the dark room, sitting on the bed with her pretty gentle face and her sad eyes, Noor was more woman than any woman Zahra had ever met.

"You were born a boy?" asked Zahra, quizzically.

"Yes, but I was always really a girl. Even the men who had sex with me in Egypt knew that I was not a boy. I just had a

112

zabr like a boy and testicles like a boy, but nothing is less of a boy than me!"

"I agree, Noor."

Zahra patted her friend's red hair and sat next to her as Noor cried all night long. She wondered if Mustafa would have realized sooner than she did that Noor was not born a woman. Mustafa had told Zahra about effeminate men who dress like women, and some of them who even wanted to be called women. He didn't seem to have any judgment for them, only sympathy for their difficult lot.

Mustafa had talked to Zahra a few times about the hardship of being a gay man in Lebanon. It was his way of making her feel less unfortunate about her colostomy.

"At least nobody takes you to jail for having a colostomy," he would say.

"I live just on the outside of society just as much as you do!" she would reply.

Noor's lot was a whole other story. Zahra felt Noor's heartbreak even as Noor fell asleep and stayed asleep until the morning. She sat next to her friend on the bed, and watched her in the light of the cutout stars.

Chapter Seventeen

The July heat reached a record high that week. No matter how torrid and exhausting the commutes got, Noor insisted they showed up to all the scheduled jobs. Zahra had to walk bare foot on burning pavement until she reached the bus one day after her plastic flip flops came apart. Noor blamed the poorly made Chinese one-dollar shoes, and promised Zahra to get her nicer ones.

"The sidewalks are cleaner than some floors we have cleaned. Consider it one of those spa treatments where they treat you with hot rocks," Noor said.

That was the only instance that made Noor giggle that week. Noor had become quiet and solemn, she stopped listening to music and would only eat a couple of bites at dinner, but only after Zahra insisted. Noor's brown eyes had dark circles, her honey skin seemed pale, and her face got thin. She eventually stopped checking her phone for texts from Hussein, who had not contacted her after he told her about his engagement.

When the phone rang one afternoon, Zahra felt her throat tighten. She hoped Hussein was calling, but the screen flashed *Anthony.* Zahra wondered if Anthony found them more apartments to clean at the building. She was glad that Noor was away at the store and couldn't be disappointed that the caller was not Hussein.

When Noor called Anthony back he told her that a pricey art sculpture was missing from the apartment belonging to Mrs. Jeha's daughter. He said that Mrs. Jeha couldn't think of anyone else besides them that had been at the apartment and wanted the two women to return the sculpture. Jeha had also made a police report, and the detective on the case asked Anthony for Noor's number.

"You walked us out, remember? Why the hell would I steal her sculpture? Her daughter's sculpture—same damn thing! What could I possibly want from her stupid sculpture?" Noor said after periods of silence where Anthony was probably explaining what was going on.

Zahra felt her stomach tighten into a knot as she gathered what was happening from Noor's responses. She couldn't remember any sculpture, as hard as she tried to recreate that apartment in her mind.

"What happened? Are we in trouble?" Zahra said when Noor hung up.

"Why would we be in trouble? Anthony let us in and let us out," Noor exclaimed. Her face was flushed red.

"Tomorrow, I will call the detective. Don't worry about it, her sculpture of *khara*. That stupid rich whore!"

It was funny to hear Noor call Mrs. Jeha names and say that the missing sculpture was made of shit. It made Zahra smile but Noor was pensive and upset, she got out of the room and told Zahra not to wait for her to sleep, that she needed to make some phone calls to try to figure out exactly what was going on.

"Are you going to call the detective now?" Zahra asked.

"The detective is fast asleep, *habibti*, do you think he has nothing besides some rich bitch's false claims to worry about?" Noor said.

Zahra wondered who Noor was going to call, but knew not to ask. She knew that Noor would have to go outside to make the calls because Diane would tap on the ceiling hard if Noor got on the phone late at night.

Zahra did not sleep well that night, and Noor did not seem to sleep at all. She came back to the room late and tossed in her bed all night. The next morning, Noor did call the detective, who requested the two girls come into the police station.

"Yes, sir, we will be there by three at the latest. Yes, three at the latest. We have to go to our job, we would lose those jobs otherwise," Noor said.

Noor didn't say a word about the detective all day or about Mrs. Jeha. Zahra felt alone in her worry, and was ready to go to the police station to get the feeling of anxiety and near panic in her throat over with. The house they cleaned that day was elegant and clean.

"When you see the painted golden pictures of Jesus in their formal room, you know they are Orthodox Christians mostly, and they all go to that big nice cathedral with huge gold-plated paintings. The richer they are, the nicer their icons get!" Noor said.

"The Muslim ones sometimes have a sura from the Koran embroidered on silk and framed," Noor added.

"Many of the Muslims here, especially the ones who want to be friends with the Americans, will do everything to hide the fact that they are Muslim. They don't pray, they don't fast—they even drink alcohol and eat pork!" Noor said.

Her spirit was coming back to her. Zahra couldn't be happier to listen and nod to her friend's recovering sarcasm after several days of silence. Zahra did not care what their customers believed in and how they showed it, the only difference between one religion and another to her was the randomness of being born into that faith. Zahra believed that humans were scared animals with flawed logic and a complex social system. Some of the people she cleaned for with Noor were kind. Most were distant and condescending. There were as many Muslim bad people to work for as there were Christian ones. Good people seemed to exist in all faiths, making Zahra believe that religion was neither necessary nor sufficient to make someone easier to work for.

Zahra did not believe in any religion. It was a lot of story and make-believe—different stories and different saviors, but illogical all the same. She knew better than to discuss religion with Noor. Instead, she nodded as her friend outlined her personal worldview. She loved Noor and wanted her to get over Hussein, the rest was unimportant as to who really lifted the sun every morning and set it down every evening.

Sami, Noor's hairdresser friend, was the one who helped them get most of the nice houses they cleaned so far. He told Noor that rich Arab immigrants copied each other in every aspect, down to the maids. He asked Noor to make sure to not tell any of the rich housewives who else they were cleaning for, and what was going on in those houses.

"Sometimes, I think that the only reason they want us to clean their houses is to find out what is going on at their friends' houses! What dinner was, who called, who stopped by and when the next dinner party is!" Noor said.

Zahra thought that using Noor as a housekeeper would be perfect, since she knew all those answers and then some beyond the nosy housewives' wildest dreams. Zahra could see why Sami would ask Noor not to repeat things she saw and heard—he probably knew his friend's affinity to gossip.

Zahra reassured Noor that she had three words for the housewives: "yes," "no," and "nothing."

When they had finished their day's work at two-thirty, the housewife of the day named Fifi asked them to stay and help with an afternoon tea hour she was hosting that day.

"I am sorry, Fifi, we can't. We have another customer at three," Noor said.

"Who is it? Call and cancel them, I will pay you double," Fifi said.

Zahra kept her eyes down and hoped Noor would handle the situation in time for them to show up at the police station when she told the detective they would.

"American, you don't know them!" Noor replied.

She assured Fifi that she could not cancel so late in the day, and that she and Zahra could return the next afternoon if Fifi wanted. Fifi gave up with a sigh and handed Noor the cash.

"Her real name is Fadwa, but she goes by to Fifi! Fadwa is too *baladi* for her! Not fancy enough!" Noor laughed.

"She wants us to stay so she can look fancy at her party, remember she came to Lulu's brunch last week, that's when she asked for our number to clean her house. Turns out she wants to show us off at her party!" Noor said.

She was referring to a social affair where Zahra and Noor helped a few days back. Zahra didn't remember seeing Fifi there, but she never looked at the women's faces or their elegant elaborate outfits. Noor did the exact opposite. She came home every day with a full detailed report of who wore what, of which housewife was trying to lose weight, and so many more details that made Zahra look forward for Ramadan ending, so she never had to see those women again.

Being around the rich housewives made Zahra tired and bored. Their voices sounded the same, their houses looked the same, and making the arguments those women got into seem even less logical. Noor updated an uninterested Zahra about the various animosities and alliances daily.

"Those women show off their maids like they show off their shoes. Lulu has a very rich husband—she is the richest one of them. That is why Fifi wants us to stay. It is all one big one up game to them. Those women don't dress up for their husbands or their kids, they dress up, put on their makeup, and wear their fancy bags to spite one another!" Noor outlined all this as they ran down the sidewalk to catch the bus to the police station.

The direct bus was gone, and they had to connect buses downtown, which made them even more late. Noor and Zahra finally got there just before four o'clock.

Chapter Eighteen

The first detective that Noor talked to had already left for the day by the time they got to the station. His replacement was a woman named Officer Marsh who asked Noor and Zahra to come into her office. The police station was nothing like the ones Zahra had seen on TV. It looked like a big office with desks on which people had pictures of their loved ones.

"Can I get you anything to drink?" the officer asked.

Both women shook their heads. The officer was wearing a police uniform.

"Do you know why you are here today, ladies?"

"Anthony said there was a robbery at the building where we worked a week ago," Noor responded.

"Yes. It happened at the apartment you two cleaned. I want to hear what you have to say about it," Officer Marsh said.

"Like what? The glass was clean, but we cleaned every window anyway, the floors were clean, but we vacuumed and mopped like she wanted us to. We are maids, not thieves!" Noor exclaimed.

The officer's face was blank. She listened to Noor's annoyed explanation. Zahra elbowed Noor, but Noor kept going.

"The concierge, Anthony, opened the door for us, he let us in and walked us out. Did you ask him if we were carrying anything? Okay, and what is missing anyway? If you are going to interrogate us like thieves how about we find out what we stole. He said some sculpture, you should see that stuff, a five-year-old with a blindfold can do better. Why would I take their ugly sculpture?" Noor was so upset her neck vein bulged and her face turned a dark red.

Zahra felt her abdomen tighten and her face heat up. A nausea rose in her chest steadier by the minute. The officer's face remained flat like the walls behind her. Officer Marsh had short, salt and pepper hair, wide shoulders, and a stocky frame. She was probably in her fifties, judging from the depth of the lines on her face and around her eyes. She looked at Zahra while Noor was going on her rant and Zahra smiled to her, apologetically, but Officer Marsh did not return the smile.

"Sit down, both of you!" she ordered and gestured to two seats across from her desk.

"I need to use the bathroom, please," Zahra interjected.

Zahra was feeling faint. It had been hot, and Noor never let them accept water in the houses they cleaned. On behalf of Ramadan, she almost killed both of them from dehydration every day. The floor was dark gray linoleum and Zahra kept staring at it to forget how sick she was feeling.

"She needs to use the restroom!" Noor snapped.

"I heard her," Officer Marsh stated.

"Where is the toilet?" Noor queried.

"She means the restroom!"

Zahra got close to Noor and hugged her from the side. Noor had lost a lot of weight, but her breasts remained inflated and perky, unaffected by grief and Ramadan. It looked like she was wearing someone else's chest. Noor's eyes were tired and her lashes had no mascara on them, her hair was dull and pulled back into a ponytail. She didn't have her usual argumentative pose with her chin up and her hand on her waist.

Zahra looked at her friend and was suddenly overwhelmed with a sadness that filled every cell of her body, Noor's fight was futile. Their dream of saving a lot of money was as unrealistic as Noor trying to prove her innocence to a detective who knew nothing about either one of them. Noor had already lost the fight, not just the fight against a detective in a police station but the fight against everything else that they pretended they could rise above: condescending housewives, and a society that had already decided what they were worth.

"Ma'am, the restroom is just around the corner. You'll see the women's sign," Officer Marsh said to Zahra in the loud exaggerated pronunciation Americans use when they think she was stupid or ignorant.

"Yes, okay." Zahra headed to the restroom.

The light turned on as soon as she opened the door. There was a mirror facing her. That's when Zahra realized that she had been crying. She emptied her bag, washed her hands and her face, and closed her eyes until she felt calm again.

When Zahra returned to Officer Marsh's desk, Noor's face was no longer red and her voice was low. She seemed calm as she smiled to Zahra. She got up, and told Zahra that they were leaving, in Arabic. She grabbed Zahra's hand and pulled her towards the door. The two women were practically running away from the station towards the bus stop.

Once they got under the bus waiting area awning, they both started laughing. The laughter got louder and harder until the bus arrived, and they sat down flushed and sweaty in the cool bus air. Noor told Zahra then how it was Mrs. Jeha who called the detective and asked that Noor and Zahra get questioned at the police station.

"She asked all her questions and I answered them, I told her one more time how Anthony walked us to the door and locked it behind us, that he saw us leave the whole building. Mrs. Jeha said we could have taken the sculpture," Noor said.

"Why did Mrs. Jeha suspect us?" Zahra asked.

"She doesn't suspect us. She wants to scare us," elaborated Noor.

"Scare us more than we are already scared of her?" Zahra said in puzzlement. They both laughed.

The bus stopped and a blond teenager with jean shorts, a purple tank, and a very pregnant belly got on and sat next to them. She didn't look at them when she sat down, but her eyes widened when Noor started talking in Arabic.

"When I was cleaning Jeha's house, I saw a framed photo of her daughter and her son-in-law. I recognized the son in law and told Sami," Noor said.

"So what if you knew her son-in-law?" Zahra was confused.

"I KNEW her son-in-law, *ya habla*!" Noor pronounced this with an undercurrent that there was more to the story.

Zahra sighed loud and the girl in braids looked once more towards them. Noor calling her stupid was ironic because Zahra was not the one who caused them to be in this predicament.

"Shhh," Zahra said, and patted Noor's hand.

Noor lowered her voice and carried on in a whisper that Zahra could barely hear.

"He was my customer once. You know, my other job, that I did before Ramadan? I am going to kill Sami, that gay *kalb*!" Noor said.

Noor called Sami a "gay dog," although he seemed up until that indiscretion to have been a good friend. He was the one who found them most of the cleaning jobs. The best paying ones were all his salon customers.

Zahra wanted to find out more, but she decided to wait until they got home. Noor was not always careful when she got upset and she sometimes said enough English words that people gathered what she was talking about. Being a thief was bad enough, but talking about prostitution was definitely not something Zahra was going to do in public.

She hugged Noor and the girl looked at them once more. This time she smiled.

Chapter Nineteen

After meeting with the detective, Noor promised Zahra not to talk about Mrs. Jeha or the incident with the police. The Arab housewives in Wichita had already found out somehow and the following days were full of disappointment for the two friends.

Every single house they were scheduled to clean turned into a cancellation, the fancy houses as well as the simple ones: the Muslims and the Christians, even the old bachelor from the Orthodox Church, who barely spoke or understood any Arabic, told Noor that he was going to start cleaning his house because he needed the exercise.

The excuses given seemed as contrived as the women delivering them. In one day the two women went from having two to three jobs a day to having none. Noor blamed Jeha and her friend Sami. Zahra attributed things to human nature.

Noor swore on her Nabi Mohamed that she would retaliate and find Zahra new customers, better and more paying ones, but both women knew that Arab patrons were not going to hire them.

As much as Zahra didn't like being talked to and asked questions by Americans, asking Beth for help finding houses to clean from First Baptist seemed like the only left option.

"Just come to church with me this Sunday and you will meet so many people, all kinds of opportunity will show up. I will pray for you to see The Lord's will for you. Everything will be fine!" Beth promised.

Zahra told her that she had plans this weekend because of Eid, but hoped to visit First Baptist and meet the men and women who prayed for her when she was still in Lebanon.

In anticipation of Eid, Noor took Zahra to the Asia Market, the Middle Eastern grocery store, that afternoon. Noor said they needed *halal* meat for Eid, not just any meat. She stored the meat in the fridge and promised to cook it the morning of Eid with eggs and spices. She haggled with the butcher, who was a young Iraqi with dark hair and a charming smile.

"This right here is my sister Zahra—not my biological sister, but I chose her to be my sister!" She pointed to Zahra and winked at the guy.

"*Ahlan* Zahra, I am Kazem," the young man offered.

"Oooh! Kazem like Kazem Al Saher? I love him! So handsome! His voice is honey! My favorite singer! *Habibi!*" Noor was flipping her hair, smiling and exclaiming all at once.

Zahra felt her cheeks get warm. She didn't really want to be introduced to anyone. Especially not a butcher at a supermarket. Noor was trying to set Zahra up with the butcher. That was why she insisted so much on Zahra coming with her to Asia Market. Zahra got close to Noor and pinched her back, and Noor laughed and pushed Zahra away.

"He likes you! See how handsome he is?" Noor said in a quiet voice.

"Shhh! *Bass!*" Zahra said, hoping Noor would stop.

Zahra was in America to get her surgery and go back to Beirut. She could continue to live with Hajji and after Hajji passes, she could pay some rent. By then she would have found

126

a job with books. She could go to college and study to be a librarian, work for a school or a college. Nadim surely needed her in his life as much as she wanted him in hers. With her colostomy repaired, Zahra could go to the beach some day with Nadim, they would sit in the sun and talk about their favorite things.

Kazem picked up on Zahra's lack of interest and went back to cutting a big slab of meat into little blocks that he piled on a big metal tray in front of him. Noor picked a jar of tahini and some spices before they head out of the store.

On their way back from Asia Market, Noor told Zahra about Hussein. She met him at that supermarket one Saturday afternoon. He asked Noor to go on a date with him that same night and she told him she was busy.

"I had a scheduled web client but even if I had nothing going on, I would have said no. I am not an easy girl! Zahra, men don't want an easy girl. I didn't even give him my number," Noor explained. She was smiling as if Hussein had just asked her moments ago to go on a date with him.

Noor seemed happy recalling the details of Hussein following her all the way back to her apartment. "I lived a couple blocks away from Asia Market at that time, and Hussein lived in that same apartment building. Can you believe my luck! I had never seen him until that day." Noor looked around, seemingly transported back to the time when Hussein wanted nobody but her.

"He said that he was going to stand in front of my building until I agreed to give him my number."

Zahra wanted to ask Noor if Hussein knew that Noor was born in a boy's body and that her legal name was that of a man, but Hussein was gone and there was no sense in making Noor upset.

"He was very jealous, so I started dressing a lot more conservatively, of course!" Noor added.

"I find that hard to believe!" Zahra snorted this response. It struck her as so funny.

They both giggled. Noor wore tight tanks and short skirts, when it was not Ramadan. She replaced the tank tops with loose T-shirts and stopped wearing makeup in her modesty initiative in honor of Ramadan.

"I still have to show what God gave me! Oh and what the plastic surgeon gave me!" Noor said and slapped her chest. "I know what you are thinking, a woman with no woman parts is never enough!"

"I didn't think that," Zahra said, defensively.

"But you wonder. Everyone who is not born like me does!" stated Noor.

Zahra shook her head. She wondered briefly, but it was the least thing she thought about, almost like questioning for a second or two why someone had a certain color of hair. She wondered a lot more about how Noor would make it now that she lost all her cleaning jobs.

"Hussein loved the way I look from my waist down. He knew what I was when he followed me. He knew when he got in my bed and he knew when he asked me to love nobody else but him," Noor sighed.

Zahra kept nodding. Soon, Noor would get to the part of Hussein leaving her and her smile would disappear, and surely there would be tears.

"He called me today, Zahra," Noor said.

"What does he want from you?" Zahra was startled.

"Exactly! I said the same thing! I told him to go call his virgin fiancée in Egypt instead!" Noor had a repulsed expression to an imaginary Hussein. She paused and studied

Zahra's expression after every sentence. "He said he loved me and couldn't get me out of his mind. He said his mother picked his bride-to-be and that he felt powerless against her choice!"

"You never mentioned his mother," Zahra said.

"He was sometimes afraid people would find out about us, about my situation. I told him I would get my surgery and then nobody would know, especially after I change my name," concluded Noor.

"Do you have to do the surgery to change your name?" Zahra asked.

"No, I was going to do the surgery for Hussein, for his family."

Zahra told Noor that she would help her find out what she needed to change her name and gender on her papers.

They were both exhausted that afternoon, Asia Market was a long walk from the bus stop. Noor was going to meet Hussein later that night. She told Zahra that Hussein was probably going to end his engagement and ask Noor to take him back.

"I am not going to make it easy for him!" Noor promised.

She put on a red sundress that accented her curves. She painted her nails a matching red and wore her hair down to the small of her back. Her heels made her look really tall, like someone on stilts, almost. Noor seemed very happy, her laughter was loud, and her eyes sparkled like they did when Zahra got to Wichita.

"I am not going to do anything that our Prophet would disagree of, it's Ramadan. I will not even kiss him, even though I am dying to. I miss him like crazy, Zahra! I will just talk to him. He seems so desperate to see me!" Noor delivered this information rapidly.

It was dark before Noor started walking away from the house. Zahra felt a knot in her stomach watching her friend disappear into the dark balancing on her pointy heels.

"Noor, *intibhi*," she yelled after her, but doubted her friend heard her tell her to be careful.

Chapter Twenty

Zahra kept woke up to a room lit by a faint daylight that mostly loitered by the small ceiling window. Noor's bed was still made. Above her head, Diane made her usual trip to the kitchen and back to the bedroom, soon the smell of coffee would sneak downstairs, and then the first cigarette smoke of the day would follow. Noor had the vent taped shut, but the house was so small and poorly ventilated that its inhabitants could smell each other's thoughts if they tried hard enough.

Zahra sat on the bed and waited until Diane got back to her bedroom to go upstairs and make sure Noor had not come home. She found no sign of Noor upstairs. Zahra's worry was turning to dread.

Noor could have spent the night with Hussein, they could have made up and for all Zahra knew, he could spend Eid with them the next day. Zahra came back downstairs and got cleaned up and dressed to go to First Baptist and talk to the refugee program coordinator about applying to Wal-Mart. Zahra planned to ask for Noor too, it would be Noor's *eidi*, her Eid gift this year. A job where people don't assume that she is good for nothing more than cleaning their toilets.

Today would be the first day Zahra rides the bus alone, she felt ready although worry about Noor kept creeping into her chest. She couldn't wait for Noor to come back to go with her, especially if the following day turned out to be an Eid they celebrated together. Noor had a long list of places to go on Eid, First Baptist was not on that list.

Zahra saw Wichita State University on her way to the church office. It was a big campus that covered two blocks, young men and women carrying bags and backpacks were walking across the streets leading to the university. Inside the gates were different buildings that Zahra imagined were different departments. She could see huge stretches of green grass and healthy colorful flowers between those buildings.

Zahra felt happy thinking about going to Wichita State someday. She would be one of those students with the pack packs crossing the street. Beth mentioned to Zahra that there was a test to take before one could qualify to become a university student, and that Beth knew refugees who took the test and got scholarships and joined Wichita State.

Zahra's heart felt full in a sunny way when she dreamed about going to the university. First, she needed her colostomy closed, the last thing she needed as a university student was an unpredictable crater that erupted randomly with repulsive smells. The bus stopped a block away from First Baptist, and Zahra's insides cramped as she remembered that Noor had not returned home. She would try to call Noor's cell from the church office, at least make sure her friend was safe.

First Baptist was a red brick building on Third Street, no gardens surrounded it like some of the other churches Zahra walked by. This was the first place she came to after Diane's house. Mary Malone introduced her to Beth that day, and Beth took Zahra to her medical appointment at the health department. It was a month ago, but seemed ages away that morning.

Inside the building lingered a sweet scent of cinnamon, it came from a room with "kitchen" on a sign by its door. Zahra didn't find anyone at the office so she sat down on a brown fabric chair with floral print.

"Zahaa! How you doing, sweetie?" A tall black lady with a large chest walked into the room. She was wearing a white tank and green pants, and her hair was pulled up into a neat bun. She stood in front of Zahra and opened her arms, gesturing a hug.

Zahra took an unsure step toward the woman. The next thing Zahra knew, she was engulfed in a warm, sweet-smelling hug that lasted a while. The woman spoke as she hugged and squeezed Zahra into her belly and chest. She patted Zahra's back like one would do to a baby.

"Honey! It is so good to see yoo! Beth been telling me you doing good, but look at yoo! You doing really good!"

The hug ended with Zahra slightly out-of-balance when the woman let go of her.

"Thank you," Zahra said. She remembered meeting the lady that first day she came, but she could not remember her name or what she did.

"I am Iris, the secretary! You been here a whole month and I did not see you!"

"I was working," Zahra said.

"Good! Very good! Beth expecting you, sweetheart? I can call her to let her know our Zahaa got here all by herself!" Iris bubbled.

Something about Iris made Zahra not mind her messing up her name. Iris felt warm and familiar, almost like home, not her mother's house but Hajji's living room when they both fell asleep in front of the television and woke up to the sound of prayer from the neighborhood mosque.

"Yes, Beth is expecting me," Zahra said. She smiled to Iris who was calling Beth.

"Yes! She's here! Yes, I tell her," Iris commented to the phone.

Iris told Zahra that Beth was on her way. "Have some cookies, sweetie, I baked them for the bible school kids!" Iris said.

"Thank you, I can't eat cookies, they hurt my stomach," Zahra said.

"No wonder you such a skinny little thing, darling! It's all right! We will find something you can eat!"

Iris asked Zahra about her month in Wichita so far, and Zahra told her about the houses they cleaned and the incident of the lady who didn't like them and about losing the houses. She told Iris that she was hoping to get a job in Wal-Mart soon. Zahra kept out the detail about Noor selling sex to Jeha's son-in-law and talking about it to her friend Sami. That reminded Zahra of Noor not coming home, and her face must have showed her worry because Iris asked her what was wrong.

"I am worried about my friend," Zahra intoned.

"Do you want to call her?" Iris asked.

Zahra used the church phone to call Noor, but Noor's phone was turned off. Zahra got the mailbox, and she left Noor a message that she was worried about her. Iris patted Zahra on the shoulder and told her that she would pray for her friend.

"Thank you Iris," Zahra said, and she meant it.

She didn't think God listened to her but if He existed, Iris seemed like the kind of woman He would listen to.

Beth showed up a half hour later and took Zahra to a computer in another room, where they looked at Wal-Mart job applications. Beth helped fill all the areas that confused Zahra. The application required two references, and Beth told Zahra that she and Iris could be her references. After filling the application, Beth and Zahra said goodbye to Iris, who made Zahra promise to come back and see her.

"And don't wait a whole month to do it!" Iris said.

Zahra promised her that she would be back soon, and she left with Beth in Jelly Belly. On the way back to Diane's, Beth stopped at McDonalds and got a number one combo. Zahra drank a Sprite while watching old men play chess at the next table.

Chapter Twenty-One

When Zahra got to the house, Diane was gone. Her keys were not by her coffee mug on the living room table. The only sound in the house was the humming of the refrigerator and the fan in Diane's room. There was still no sign of Noor.

Zahra got her grocery bag from the pantry. She spread some soft cheese on a piece of pita and sat down to eat it. The first bite barely made it past her tightened throat into a cramping stomach. Zahra looked around at the small kitchen, hoping to find an answer.

She didn't know Noor's friends, only heard about them. Diane did not allow the women to have visitors and, besides, they were busy working most of the time. Zahra remembered the name of the hairdresser: Sami, like the name of a kid she went to grade school with.

She closed her eyes and tried to imagine Sami's face, the Sami from her childhood who had curly hair and olive skin, big brown eyes and a sly smile. Zahra thought about where that Sami was today—probably married with a handful of kids.

Zahra wondered if everyone from her childhood had gone on to have a grown-up life besides her. Her accident made time stand still. She stood on the outside and watched people go on with their lives. The only sign that they could see her sitting outside their circle were their expressions and their remarks when they saw her. Most people in her neighborhood heard about the missile attack that almost killed her. The rumors that went around and somehow got back to Zahra were worse than the actual injury.

People said that Zahra was disfigured from the attack, some said she was paralyzed. Both stories were true. The accident had disfigured her and paralyzed her from participating to life with those people, but as far as they could tell, Zahra still looked the same. Her scars were under her shirt and her schedule of caring for a colostomy was not evident to anyone who didn't know her well.

Despite looking like any normal young woman from a distance, Zahra was no longer one of the normal people. People knew even before she did that she was a freak, someone who had to hide to avoid pity. The only two people who didn't seem to realize that Zahra was stuck outside society were Hajji and Mustafa, perhaps because they themselves were outcasts, just like her.

Zahra hated how people seemed to know that Hajji had lost her mind without even having to talk to her, and that Mustafa was effeminate without ever getting to know him. Zahra saw the way people who didn't know them looked at Hajji and Mustafa. In her case, it was the people who knew her, or of her, who's judging eyes penetrated her loose black shirt and exposed her scarred abdomen and her colostomy bag.

Sami the hairdresser was a faceless man who found them the better paying cleaning jobs. Zahra could not remember his last name or where he worked; she was not sure Noor even mentioned either. Zahra knew that talking to Sami would upset Noor. Anyone worrying about Noor would upset her too, but Zahra was past the point of worry.

Noor mentioned many times how much she hated when people gossiped about her. Sometimes Zahra wondered why Noor lived with the choices she lived with when she craved privacy. It was hard not to stare at Noor's red hair, her tall slender body, and large breasts. Until the beginning of Ramadan, Noor always wore tight fitting tanks that were cut low enough to reveal too much chest. Noor acted revolted when men stared but the spring in her step and the backwards flip of her hair which followed said otherwise.

Zahra felt the pit in her stomach get deeper as she recalled Noor's pretty face. She knew that Noor was not back because something bad had happened. The worst part of the fear Zahra felt in her dry throat was not knowing where to start looking for Noor, or what to tell people about why Noor left the previous night. Doing nothing about her friend's disappearance was the only thing worse than explaining the circumstances to strangers in her heavily accented English, which people seemed to struggle to understand.

Zahra rested her head on the plastic cover with the pink and green pattern on the small breakfast table, she closed her eyes for a few seconds. Noor's perfume lingered around the kitchen like regret.

At that moment, Zahra remembered that Noor used to live in an apartment building next to Asia Market and that was where she met Hussein. As hard as she tried, Zahra couldn't remember the stops to get to the Asian Market. She closed her eyes again, and tried to retrace the last bus trip she did with Noor. She decided to go to the bus stop three blocks from the house and ask someone waiting there about Asia Market. Anyone with a phone could help her figure out the street intersection and then she could find the right buses to get her there.

Zahra locked the door and started walking. She kept hoping that Noor would be heading back, and she would see her. Zahra thought of all the stories she would tell Noor once she found her; how she took the bus alone and found the church, how she was waiting to hear from Wal-Mart, how she found her own way to Asia Market. Zahra imagined Noor's expression and her exclamations that would follow the story of that day.

When Zahra got to the nearest bus stop, she was the only person waiting. She felt the panic in her stomach again. Her plan so far was not going as she imagined it would. She thought about going inside a store and asking. The bus got to the stop and Zahra got on it and asked the driver how to get to Asia Market.

The driver couldn't understand Zahra's accent. Twice he asked her where she was going, and twice she replied "Asia Market." Everyone on the bus was staring at Zahra and the driver.

"This bus does *not go* to Asia Market. Buses stop at intersections, not Asian markets, miss," the driver explained.

"I know, but where is it? I am trying to find my friend," Zahra said.

"I have no idea where your friend is, miss! You have to find out the streets and then get on the right bus. I don't have time for this!" he said. His voice was loud and his face angry. He looked at two of his passengers and said, "They come to this country and they can't understand English! I am not *Google Maps*!"

The passengers looked at Zahra, waiting for her to answer the accusations. She turned away and got off the bus.

There was a gas station down the street. Zahra walked towards it without looking behind her. She opened the door to a chime and felt the cool air inside.

She thought about how she understood English better than the loud driver, who didn't know the first thing about her. She wished she could tell him that she has a right to be in America as much as he does, even more than he did. His country made bombs and sold them for money and people like her got injured and ended up somewhere having to learn a new way to live.

Zahra took a deep breath and pushed her tears back in. She opened the fridge door and grabbed a cold bottle of water, paid for it, and walked back into the midday heat.

She drank her water on the sidewalk in front of everyone. Noor was not with her to stop her on behalf of Ramadan. She felt mad at Noor, and worried about her all at once.

She walked back to the bus station and headed to First Baptist this time.

Chapter Twenty-Two

"Well look what the cat just dragged in *again*! Did you forget something, honey?" Iris exclaimed. She laughed and opened her arms for Zahra, who initiated the hug this time.

Zahra started in. "Noor, my friend, she is not at home yet. I am worried very much for her safety," Zahra said.

Iris listened intently and nodded her head. Her expression got progressively more concerned as Zahra told her more.

Zahra kept out the details of Noor being transgender, and of Hussein having left her for an Egyptian bride that his mother picked for him. She was not sure if telling Iris that would change anything. What mattered was that her friend left the night before, hadn't come back home yet, and that her phone was dead.

Iris had Zahra repeat some sentences because she couldn't understand what Zahra meant. When Iris understood something the second time, after Zahra repeated it, she would typically laugh and say, "Oh yes, yes, yes! I missed that! You did say that!" sounding like an adult who was thrilled to hear a toddler talk and was encouraging them to say more.

"Should we go looking for your friend, sweetie?" Iris said, her words stretched and sincere.

Zahra told Iris that they had to go to Asia Market that was the last place she went to with Noor.

"Let me look this Asian place up, what's it called, you say?" Iris asked.

They headed to Asia Market in Iris' car, which was located at the intersection of Twenty-First and Woodlawn, according to Iris' phone book. Iris' car was a white Toyota with an inside that smelled like pine. She told Zahra to roll her window down, because the air conditioning was not working at the moment. When they pulled into the parking lot, Iris said she recognized the place, because she had given rides to people from the refugee program who went there and got their groceries and sometimes walked to the hair salon next door, where some got their hair braided.

Iris came into the store with Zahra and followed her to the meat case.

Kazem got up and walked towards Zahra with a big smile.

"*Ahlan, ahlan!*" he said with a big smile on his face. His expression and voice trailed off when he realized Zahra was not smiling back.

"I am looking for Noor. She went to see Hussein last night and has not come home since. I tried calling her, her phone is dead," Zahra told Kazem in Arabic.

Kazem looked at Iris to see if she understood what was going on, but Iris was looking at the grocery isle behind him.

"*Wayn* Hussein?" Zahra asked Kazem, hoping he would know who Hussein was and where he was.

"*Baddik trouhi hinak?*" he asked her.

Zahra nodded and Kazem told her he would take her to Hussein's apartment, but couldn't leave the meat section right away. He explained that tomorrow was Eid, and that it would be at least another couple hours before he could step away.

Surely enough, a short heavy woman came towards them and had a list of different kinds of meats she wanted. Kazem

142

glanced at Zahra in a "see?!" expression, and got busy cutting the meat on the block. The customer quickly realized that Zahra and Iris were not waiting for their meat order and scanned them with curious eyes. Her long shapeless dress covered most of her and was the color of a cloudy day. It matched her skin and the headscarf she wore, her monochromatic tights showed just above her ankle and blended into plain dusty shoes. The woman reminded Zahra of the insects that blend with tree bark to avoid getting eaten by birds.

Iris smiled to the lady and said, "Hi!" The lady looked Iris up and down and turned her looks away after mumbling something that sounded more like "hhhh."

"Come on, explain to me what's on those shelves!" Iris said to Zahra and gently pushed Zahra away from the butcher department. Zahra reluctantly walked with Iris, who said, "We be right here when you got a minute," to Kazem. Iris smiled once more to the customer, who now looked five hundred times more curious to figure out what was happening.

"He said he needs two hours," Zahra told Iris.

"No, he don't. I will go talk to the man upfront and explain we don't got all day to find that poor girl."

When Iris said "explain" it sounded like "sssplayn," and Zahra nodded.

Kazem got into Iris' car with both women and showed them the way to Hussein's apartment. It was just down the street, like Noor said. Noor had told Zahra about the early days of her romance with Hussein. When had he been Noor's neighbor, he watched her walk to the bus stop down the street every day. Iris asked Zahra if she needed her to walk to Hussein's apartment with her. Zahra shook her head, "no."

143

"I be right here, darling." Zahra saw worry in the brown of Iris' eyes and the gentle nod she gave her.

Zahra and Kazem took one flight of stairs and he pointed to a door that looked no different than a bedroom door, with a metal number *twenty-one* on it.

Kazem knocked twice on the door, then looked at Zahra and shook his head.

"Do you know this, Hussein? Can you call him?" Zahra asked.

"He probably doesn't want people getting in his business," Kazem said.

"I don't care about his business, my friend has been gone since last night, do you want me to call the police?" Zahra responded.

"Listen, I know him on Facebook, we are not close friends or anything. I can message him on Facebook and call you if he answers. Just leave your number and I will call you. I have to get back to work!"

Zahra walked back to the car and told Iris that Kazem knocked and nobody answered, and that he was going to check on Facebook. Iris got out of the car and walked towards Kazem who was leaving the parking lot in the direction of Asia Market.

"Where do you think you are going young man?" Iris demanded.

"Listen, lady, I got nothing to do with this guy and his tranny, it's their shit to figure out! I have to get back to work," Kazem said, his voice loud and his eyes dark with anger.

"Oh, is that right? If this was your sister, would you want some noble man just like you to leave her in danger?!" Iris was yelling right back at Kazem, whose face got dark and neck veins filled up.

"You don't even know what you are getting yourself into! Don't mention my sister in the same sentence as a freak! My sister is a virgin, one who doesn't put ads for her body on the Internet!" Kazem yelled. "This Noor you are looking for is a man, did she tell you that!" he said, pointing towards Zahra.

Iris stood right in front of Kazem as he tried to move past her and leave. He was shorter than Iris, but seemed capable of hurting her. Zahra hated Kazem more than she hated anyone, even Mrs. Jeha. She was too scared to open her mouth, she stood behind Iris shaking.

"Tell you what, I am not saying this again, you go back to that door and call your friends, or I am calling the police on your ass!" Isis asserted, using an extended finger to accent each of her points.

Something about Iris not moving and yelling louder than Kazem made him go back to the apartment door and start kicking it like a mad man. He screamed in Arabic to Hussein to open the door before he kicked it open, and that he didn't want his name associated with a male prostitute. The door opened and a man with a beard in white underwear stood behind it.

"Here is the dog you are looking for!" Kazem yelled as he walked away gesturing, cussing. He stomped down the stairs to head back to the Asia Market.

Iris walked right into the apartment and Zahra followed her.

Chapter Twenty-Three

Hussein stood in his underwear staring at Zahra and Iris. His eyes were bloodshot, his hands to his sides partly opened like someone asking "what?" A few seconds passed with him in front of them, looking confused and scared at once. He smelled like alcohol and exhaustion, the way people do when they have not eaten for days. He started to say something that turned into a cry, it sounded more like an injured animal than a human.

The apartment was a tiny living room with a sofa and a television and a dinette set next to what looked like a big window connected to a kitchenette. Zahra could see a mostly empty bottle of liquor of some sort on the table, no glasses.

Noor would not drink from a bottle, was the first thought that came to Zahra's mind. In the corner of the living room was an open door, through which Zahra saw Noor's red dress on the floor. She ran towards the dress as Hussein's shrieks got louder. In a dim bedroom, on a messed-up bed among the sheets, was Noor, naked and unconscious.

Zahra jumped on the bed and starting shaking Noor, who made a whimper and kept her eyes closed. Zahra didn't realize that she was screaming until Iris stood next to her and held her.

"I called the police, it's gonna be alright, darling, you making her more scared with your hollering like that, calm down, Zahaa!"

Iris then walked into the bathroom and took a washcloth that she wet and brought back to Noor's face. Noor had cuts and bruises all over her, her left eye was swollen with red and blue all over that side of her face. Her lips were cut and blood framed her usually white teeth. Noor's breasts seemed huge with the rest of her naked body, her skin was pale and felt cold. Noor's left nipple was crusted with blood and a bruise that looked like a bite next to it. There were bruises in the shape of lines that ended with a rectangular scab all over Noor's flat stomach and long legs.

Between Noor's legs was a small penis and dangling testicles that looked a little larger than a little boy's. A long dry line of blood went from the unconscious girl's knee up her right thigh into the space between her legs. Clumps of Noor's long hair were scattered all over the bed.

Iris lifted Noor gently and rested her head on her lap while she gently wiped down Noor's face. Noor whimpered every time Iris moved the cloth.

"I know darling, I know," Iris kept saying, she shushed Noor and told her she was right here and everything was going to be okay.

Zahra cried and squeezed Noor's hand until the paramedics arrived and put Noor on a stretcher with an oxygen mask covering her face. The police officers arrived next, and that's when Zahra and Iris realized that Hussein had left the apartment. The police car was still parked outside after the ambulance left with Noor.

The detective told Iris that they needed to ask Zahra some questions, after which she could go to the hospital to be with her friend.

"She can't answer no questions right now, can't you see how shaken that child is!" Iris told the officer who looked at Zahra and asked her to please follow him.

Zahra told the officer that she didn't know Hussein's last name or phone number, and that she had never met him. He asked her if her friend had been drinking before she left the house, and she told him that Noor never drank the entire time Zahra knew her, and besides, it was Ramadan when Noor didn't go out at all.

"But she was clearly out the night she didn't come back," the officer stated.

"Yes, she went out to talk to Hussein, he asked her to meet him," Zahra said. She felt like her face was on fire, she fought her tears back.

The officer acted as if Noor had done something wrong. He asked Zahra about the work she did with Noor and how much they got paid. Zahra finally got quiet and answered either "yes" or "no." She was exhausted and couldn't understand English very well. She was mixing Arabic with her English and her colostomy was feeling very full.

"I have to go," she said to the officer.

"Keep your eyes open for the man who attacked your friend. If you hear from him, or if he stops by the hospital give me a call, here is my card," the officer said as he handed her a business card.

"He hurt her really bad, I thought he killed her!" Zahra said.

"Yes, that's what you keep saying. We will talk to your friend when he wakes up." The officer put a comforting hand on Zahra's shoulder.

Zahra looked at Iris to see if she heard the officer call Noor a "he." Zahra knew that Noor had not changed her name and

148

gender because she was still unsure how to do it, but anyone could see that Noor was not a "he." Zahra knew that she would be betraying her friend if she let the officer continue to refer to her as a man.

"My friend is a woman, she is a she. Soon her identity card will change," Zahra said.

"When that happens, ma'am, I will call your friend a she. For right now I have a male-bodied person with "male" as the gender on the driver's license. I hope you can understand." The policeman gestured to Zahra that she could leave and started to walk towards his car.

"What this young woman is telling you, officer, is what you need to hear. We got here and found her almost dead!" Iris said. Her tone was sad.

The officer didn't answer Iris.

"Let's go to the hospital, sweetheart, your friend is going to need us there, *especially* if everybody caring for *her* is a close-hearted asshole like this man."

Iris was still shaking her head when she got into her car and they headed towards Wesley hospital where Noor would be, according to the paramedics.

Chapter Twenty-Four

Daylight had turned into night by the time Zahra was able to see Noor.

Iris refused to leave Zahra alone in the emergency room. She took Zahra across the street to a sandwich place, and bought her a turkey sandwich with lettuce, tomatoes, and a pickle on the side. Zahra stared at the sandwich and cried for a long time before eating a couple of bites. Every time Zahra saw the sandwich, the image of Noor with blood filling her mouth came to her mind and made her weep.

Zahra had not even emptied her colostomy since the middle of the day, but she had not had anything to eat or drink and had even entirely forgotten about having the bag.

Iris held Zahra's hand and prayed for Noor. People could see Iris praying, but she didn't seem to care, Iris didn't seem to care about most things she did in front of people. Zahra knew her for one day and she was already feeling brave by being around her. Iris' presence felt like a shield that kept the world at bay.

"Heavenly Father full of Grace, we thank you for the gift of this day and the gift of Zahaa and Noor. We ask you to heal Noor's injuries and mend her broken heart. Keep her in your heavenly watch and help her Lord, help her! Help the world see her for who she is and help her find your way. We trust

You know what is best for all of us! In Jesus' name, amen!" Iris' eyes were squeezed shut while she prayed, she squeezed Zahra's hands in rhythm with her conversation with God and nodded every time she added something to God's "to-do list" for Noor.

When she opened her eyes, Zahra said, "Thank you very much."

Iris' version of God didn't bother Zahra. Happy endings seemed possible despite a whole lot of suffering in Iris' world. Zahra believed Iris' promises of better days. She held on to that belief even though her own faith in everything else was close to nonexistent.

Zahra knew the nurse was calling for her when she heard Noor's birth name; "Abbas Hadi's family," called out the woman in scrubs.

Iris missed the whole thing but followed Zahra into the emergency room cubicle. Noor's eyes were swollen near shut but she seemed awake. Zahra got close to her bed and took her hand. Noor sniffled and looked away from the two women.

"I am gonna be waiting outside for you, child, come get me if you need me," Iris said. She left Zahra alone with Noor.

"*Habibti* Noor, *salamtik.*" Wishing Noor well seemed wishful.

"He was drunk when I got there. He blamed me for everything! He said I made him sick like me! He called me all the names that ever existed. He *hit* me, Zahra!" Noor's words sounded like hiccups between loud sobs.

"I told the police officer, they will put him in jail," Zahra said.

"No, Zahra, they will believe him and blame this on me! I told him I didn't go there to have sex. He said that sex was the

151

only thing I was good for!" Noor wept as she looked away from her friend.

Noor's nurse entered the room, she informed Noor that she was cleared to go home as long as she followed up with her doctor the next morning. Noor nodded and asked the nurse if she could keep the hospital gown.

"I don't have anything else to put on," Noor said, her voice forlorn.

Iris went to First Baptist and came back with clothes for Noor. She refused to let Noor leave the hospital with a gown that showed most of her body. While Iris was gone, Zahra told Noor about her day, about Iris helping her.

"She is a good woman," explained Zahra.

"She saved my life," Noor said.

Noor left the hospital wearing a pink tank top over a nice bra and matching underwear, with brand new jeans and leather pumps. Iris made the nurse get her a brush and Noor looked much better by the time they all got in the car. They went to a drive-through and got Noor a strawberry milk shake

"To match your pretty pink hair and your outfit!" said Iris. Her resonant laughter returned.

She dropped Noor and Zahra off at Diane's and promised to return first thing in the morning.

"Tomorrow is Eid; the feast we celebrate at the end of Ramadan. I promised Noor we would go out, maybe you can join us!" Zahra said.

Noor smiled, her eyes tired and surrounded by bruises.

"For sure, darling! Let's get our show on the road!" Iris said. She gave Zahra one of her big hugs and Noor a more gentle one.

"This girl right here gonna take good care of you, everything's gonna be just fine, sweetie, I'll see your pretty face in the morning, get you some rest!" Iris patted Noor on the shoulder and gave Zahra an affectionate look.

Noor and Zahra went down to their room. It was still lit by the small lamp with the cutout stars, Zahra's bed was still not made in contrast with Noor's bed with the pink velvet comforter neatly covering it.

Noor asked Zahra to sit next to her in the bed. She told Zahra every time she closed her eyes, she saw Hussein whipping her with his belt and pulling her hair. She was crying again when she said that.

Zahra got in bed with Noor and gently stroked her hair. Every once in a while, Noor would wince and involuntarily push Zahra's hand away. They laid there for about an hour, neither one able to sleep,

"We don't know for sure if tomorrow is Eid," Noor said.

"If the new moon shows up, it is," Zahra said.

"Let's find the new moon." Noor got out of bed, put on her house slippers, and slowly walked up the stairs.

Zahra and Noor sat on the concrete step that led to Diane's front door. They both looked up to a sky with a handful of faint stars. An occasional faint breeze snuck between houses. It was mostly still, yet the night felt refreshing after the long day it followed.

The entire block was dark. People slept in their small houses with peeling paint, humming window units, and messy yards. An occasional dog bark made its way into an otherwise quiet dark. Zahra closed her eyes and imagined Diane's house gone, and the neighboring houses gone too. She pretended that they were in a world where poor neighborhoods did not exist, where she did not have a colostomy, and Noor was born with all the right parts.

"I tried being a boy, but it never worked, not even for an hour, not even when I got whipped. I hated myself more than anyone could possible ever hate me," Noor shared.

"The only way someone can hate you, Noor, is not knowing you. You are impossible to hate." Zahra stated this with conviction.

"Most of the time I feel impossible to love," Noor said, her tears replaced by a desolate exhaustion.

"I know, me too," agreed Zahra.

Zahra couldn't see much of her friend in the dark but she could hear her quiet breath. She closed her eyes and imagined Beirut that dawn; the end of Ramadan celebrated with Koran prayers resonating from neighborhood mosque towers. Zahra didn't care for the muezzin's multiple daily calls for prayer. Nadim told her how he missed the sound of azan when he was in America; she told him then that she wouldn't.

On that porch however, covered in dark, Zahra wished the muezzin's sad resolved call for prayer covered her and drowned the sound of her heart breaking.

"I see it!" Noor said, pointing, her voice a whisper.

Above them, a slice of moon was undeniable. It came out of nowhere and claimed a spot in the black sky. Zahra smiled to it and so did Noor.

Chapter Twenty-Five

The sun's rays entering the small daylight window in the room indicated it was close to noon. Zahra had learned the dance of daylight and time on Noor's alarm clock the first week she got to Wichita. The hours dragged until Beth showed up to take Zahra to her appointments.

She had forgotten about what happened the previous day until she saw Noor's hair peeking from under her covers in the bed across the room. Noor was still asleep. Iris said she was coming to celebrate Eid with them. Zahra hoped that she would show up soon. There had been too much pain and loss to face. Iris made it a little better.

Zahra got out of her bed quietly and got cleaned up and dressed in the bathroom. She still had not changed in front of Noor, and until yesterday Noor had never been naked in front of Zahra either. When Zahra returned to the bedroom, Noor was sitting in the bed and smiling at her.

"Eid Mubarak, Zahra!" Noor said. Her face was black and blue, her lips were swollen, and she still had some blood between her teeth. Zahra tried not to show her shock. Her tears surged like a river in the spring.

She squeezed her eyes as tight as she could while smiling back to her friend. "Eid Mubarak, Noor!"

The doorbell rang and they heard Diane's footsteps above. Zahra sprung upstairs trying in vain to beat Diane to the door. A smiling Iris wearing a hot pink skirt and a matching blouse with ruffles stood at the door, smiling at Diane. Zahra started to explain that Iris was just there for a few minutes and then they would all go celebrate Eid at the mall, when Iris walked right into the living room and gave Zahra one of her warm hugs.

"Well, happy holiday, darling! I am sorry I don't know how to pronounce the words in y'all's language! You gonna have to work with me a little bit on that!"

Diane didn't oppose Iris' presence in her living room. Zahra was not sure how she escaped the "no visitor" rule, but the next thing she knew, Iris was sitting on Diane's sofa, visiting with Diane. Diane never talked to anyone, but seemed to be willing to answer Iris' questions about how she watered her lawn, how close she was to paying off the house, and the outrageous price of gas. Diane even offered Iris a cup of coffee, which Iris declined on account of saving her appetite for the food court.

"Look at you girl! Don't you look A-MAZIN'?" Iris was practically screaming, her face beamed.

Zahra and Diane turned around and there was Noor standing at the top of the stairs, in a satin dress with spaghetti straps and a white belt at the waist, which matched her high-heeled sandals. Her bruises were covered by makeup, her eyelids were perfectly painted, and her lashes looked thick and long with wingtips at the edges that reminded Zahra of Cleopatra's pictures in books. Noor's lips, eyelids, and dress, in different shades of peach made her look like a model from a magazine.

"Well, aren't you just fancy!" Diane said.

"It's our holiday, Eid-al-Fitr, the festival of breaking Ramadan fast," Noor said.

"Good thing you two broke fast all along! If you will excuse me, I got some crocodile hunting to catch up on!" Diane said in a laugh that ended in a staccato cough. Diane got up and went to her room where she usually lit a cigarette and watched TV.

"We got some partying to do girls! Let's hustle!" Iris said.

Zahra put on her shoes and they headed to Town West Mall. Iris told them that first they had to get some makeup on Zahra, "So people don't think you been kidnapped before you got a chance to get ready!" Zahra insisted that she didn't like makeup and had never worn it.

"Just as well!" Iris said, and kept heading towards the makeup counter in one of the department stores. "My friend Linda gone fix you up, doll! You just sit on the chair and stay still!"

Noor nodded, excited about the idea, and Zahra went along with it for her friend's sake.

Linda worked on Zahra's face for some time, Noor suggested the colors and the makeup style. Zahra saw a side of Noor she had not encountered before, a Noor that was focused and self-assured. When Linda was done, she handed Zahra a mirror.

Zahra didn't look like herself. She could pass for someone with a perfect life and a perfect past. Her face with makeup made her baggy T-shirt and black sweats look like someone else's clothes.

The three women were grinning as they watched Zahra look at her reflection.

"See what I tell you! I know that pretty face of yours could use some putting together," Iris said.

Zahra asked Linda how much money she owed.

"Zero dollars and zero cents! Iris is my childhood friend. It's my pleasure, especially because Iris says it's a holiday where you guys come from," Linda declared.

Linda then asked them where they were working, and Zahra told her that she was waiting to hear back from Wal-Mart because their house cleaning job was not going as well as they thought it would.

"What about your young lady?" Linda asked Noor.

"I was cleaning houses with Zahra," Noor replied.

"Forget about housekeeping! You should come work for me. You got good makeup skills, look at that pretty face of yours. You are an artist! I bet you are a good salesperson too," Linda added.

"Girl she can sell ice cubes to the Eskimos! Don't let that shy smile of hers fool you!" Iris said.

She had never met Noor until the day that she walked into Hussein's apartment and rescued her with Zahra.

Linda took Noor's number after they agreed to meet after Eid was over.

People were staring at Zahra more than they ever had, it made her feel awkward no matter how beautiful Iris and Noor told her she was. She excused herself to go to the bathroom and washed the makeup off. When she got back to the food court, Iris and Noor were standing in line in front of the pizza place. Iris insisted on paying. Noor picked a slice of cheese pizza and Zahra got breadsticks. Iris got two slices of pepperoni pizza, "in case somebody wanted to share."

"We cannot eat pepperoni, it is made of pork meat, haram in our religion, against the rules," Noor said.

Zahra's face turned red. She didn't want Noor to hurt Iris's feelings, not after everything Iris had done for them.

"Ah, well then, the more pizza for me!" Iris said and laughed. Noor smiled to her and they started talking about Noor working at the makeup counter. Noor's spirits seemed to be returning to her, she still moved slow and winced every once in a while when she moved.

After the food court, the three women looked at clothes and shoes for a couple hours. Zahra hated being around clothes that she could not wear, she was more than willing to look at clothes that day, because Noor and Iris seemed to enjoy looking at and talking about fashion. Noor suggested they go to a movie at the Palace since it was so close, and it was too hot to do anything outside. Iris agreed, and they decided to watch a comedy titled *Bad Moms,* about moms who decide to take a break from their families. The movie made Iris and Noor laugh quite a bit. Zahra was happy because Noor seemed to be recovering.

The day ended with ice cream from McDonalds and a car ride down the highway with the windows down and Nancy Ajram's music up. The music came from Noor's playlist, which Iris connected to her car with a special cable. The music was Iris's idea. She wanted to have an Eid the way "y'all would," and Noor told her that music was the missing piece.

Noor sang whole songs one after another, and Iris shook her head to the rhythm with her fingers spreading out then clinching back onto the beige stirring wheel. When the car stopped in front of Diane's house with the music blasting out of the windows, Zahra realized she was clapping her hands and smiling so hard her face hurt. It was the best Eid she had ever had.

"Let's do this again next Eid!" Iris said with her customary laughter.

When Noor and Zahra walked into the house, Diane told them that a detective stopped by the house, she handed them his card.

"If you are getting in trouble, I want you out of my house. Both of you."

"Diane, we are not in any trouble, somebody attacked me, and he wants to talk about it. I am going to start a job at the mall, corporate, I am hoping to pay five more dollars per week to help with utilities like you wanted me to."

"What are you going to do when she works at the mall?" Diane asked Zahra. Her tone was skeptical of the story Noor told.

"She is going to work in retail too, not sure when she starts. It may take her more time to get through the process," Noor answered.

Zahra nodded to Diane's verifying looks.

Before she got in bed, Noor washed off her makeup. Her bruises looked darker but her spirits remained light. The bounce in her step assured Zahra that her friend's spirit escaped the abuse her body had endured.

"Zahra *inti oukhti*! I have never had a sister," Noor said, she was crying.

"*Inti oukhti Kaman*," Zahra responded. She had sisters, unlike Noor, but she felt closer to Noor than she did to any of them.

"Tomorrow we will go get jobs and the dirty Arabs can clean their own houses. We are too good to be stuck in this basement. When Allah wants His worshiper's dream to come true, no man can stop us," Noor exclaimed.

Zahra cried under her covers. She hoped Noor's God was done with the torturous phase and that indeed He had a break in store for her friend. Noor's soft, rhythmic sleep, with the stars illuminating the ceiling seemed the closest thing to hope that Zahra had experienced in a while.

She felt sleep slip under her eyelids. Her thoughts seemed so clear that they felt like a letter someone was reading to her.

America made the bomb that took Zahra's insides and kept her in the hospital for a year. When she was ready to go home, Zahra had no home to go to. Nadim became her family. America took him from her when she left Lebanon five weeks ago. As the stars lulled her to sleep, Zahra wondered if America was really to blame for her suffering. In her half-asleep mind, she considered if it was not a combination of coincidence and bad luck that took her life from her until now. The same America she blamed for so long was going to give Zahra her life back. She was going to write her own story and create the ending she wanted.

Chapter Twenty-Six

Summer heat broke in a storm that lasted a week. When the sun finally came back on Saturday, it seemed penitent and transformed into a source of pleasant warmth. In front of a yellow bungalow, Iris kneeled in her yard pulling weeds from an opulent lawn. A car pulled into her driveway, she waved expectantly at a dressed-up Noor in high heels. Noor walked hurriedly towards the house.

"Zahra is coming over for dinner, just push that oven back on, I still got the rolls to bake, you know how she loves some fresh-baked bread," Iris said.

Noor mumbled something as she entered the house. She was tired after her day of work at the makeup counter, her feet hurt from standing long hours. She was very excited to see Zahra.

Noor set up the table with the pink ceramic dishes and cups she bought with her employee discount at the mall. Noor took a step back from the table and smiled, pleased with her work. She would prepare *koshary* to serve with Iris' pot roast and bread rolls, but first she needed to change so that her nice work clothes didn't pick up the scent of fried onions. Noor walked into her bedroom and carefully took her suit off, put it on a wooden hanger, and set it back in her closet. She stood in front of the mirror and checked her profile. Her spandex underwear was restricting her, so she slipped it off and pulled a loose cotton pair from the drawer.

Noor looked at the mirror again; her penis hung soft, its tip reaching just below her testicles. She put her hand over it, pushed it inside the sac the way she had done many times to pretend it was not there. The skin folds that she made with the pressure would be her vagina someday. She could see how a surgery was possible and would put an end to the years she lived in the wrong body. She released her hand and looked down again once more. Her shaft was hard. Noor smiled at the pleasurable fullness she felt between her legs.

"You will lose the ability to orgasm from what used to be a penis. Right now, the hormones you are on affect that anyway," Dr. Meineke had said.

He was the plastic surgeon she drove three days to see in New York City. At that time, Noor told the surgeon that she wanted a vagina, even if it meant she never climaxed again. She would use her mermaid body as long as she needed to and, after it made thirty thousand dollars, she would be able to transform into a princess Hussein could marry. Her transformation would be more for Hussein's family than for him—nobody should find out about her past. Hussein loved her body the way he found it, he was bewitched by her sorceress parts, and spent hours at her altar earning her love.

Hussein killed himself the day he hurt Noor, the neighbor found him hanging from a rope tied to a pipe in the basement.

Noor put on the rest of her clothes and left the room.

Iris picked some roses from her garden for the dining table. Pink and red roses stood in the vase adding more color to the table. Iris took her apron off, washed her hands, and got busy finishing up the meal. Next to her stood Noor by the stove.

She heated some oil in a saucepan, then added a chopped onion and stirred it. She kept moving the onions around the pan until they turned a light brown and filled the kitchen with aroma. Noor then added the rice and lentils and walked away from the stove after covering her now bubbling pan. When the lentils and rice softened, Noor added pasta and cubed, homegrown tomatoes that Iris had prepared on top of the dish. She then placed on the table. Zahra was always on time, she would be walking down the block from the bus stop and turning into their street any minute.

"Remind me to send some garden vegetables with her," Iris said.

"She can't eat a lot of vegetables, she hardly eats at all," confided Noor.

"It shows, she is a sack of bones! I can't wait until that poor thing gets her surgery."

Iris saw Zahra from her kitchen window and she hurried outside to meet her. "Well look what the cat dragged in!"

Zahra smiled and hugged Iris, who showed Zahra all the strawberries and tomatoes in the garden before they came inside.

"The food is getting cold!" Noor proclaimed. She hugged Zahra too, and gestured both of them to the table.

At the table, Noor talked about her day at work. She had been living with Iris for two months and working at the mall for six weeks. Diane kicked her out after police and a social worker showed up to the house to talk to Noor about Hussein's suicide.

The move was good for Noor, and it turned out to be just as good for Iris. A little over a year before Zahra and Noor met Iris, her daughter Dawn was sent to prison. Iris didn't say much about Dawn, but Noor told Zahra whatever story she put together from the bits and pieces she heard from Iris and the people who came to visit her. Noor drove Iris' car because Iris got nervous driving long distances, and they went to visit Dawn every other Monday. Both Noor and Iris were off on Mondays, so they drove three hours each way to go to the Oklahoma City Prison, where Dawn was sentenced to ten years for selling and using drugs.

Iris always cried when she talked about her daughter. She said she was glad "her baby" didn't die and that she trusted Jesus would fix everything. Zahra thought it was a big mess to fix, but she loved Iris and agreed with her that Jesus indeed could help. *At least Jesus helped Iris wait for the ten years to pass,* Zahra thought.

Iris blamed herself for working all the time and missing the "signs," but that was all ten years ago because Dawn ran away from home when she was seventeen. Iris didn't hear from her except when she got in trouble with the law.

"I kept bailing her out, until one day her crime was too big for me to fix. She had gotten herself into a mess with a man who used Dawn for prostitution and selling drugs."

Noor told Zahra that Dawn was a nice girl, tall, but otherwise looked nothing like Iris. She always asked her mom for Twinkies, Cheetos, and phone minutes. Dawn never called Iris with the phone money.

"I think she calls that drug dealer boyfriend who landed her in jail," Noor said. She told Zahra that Allah sent Iris to her and her to Iris.

After dinner, the three women sat on the front porch on blue plastic chairs. Kids played on the street. Some of them were on bicycles, and others chased after each other. Iris had lived in that house since Dawn was five years old.

"When does your summer class end, Zahra?" Iris asked.

"One more week," Noor answered for Zahra. Although Noor was a year younger than Zahra, she acted like her big sister and felt compelled to answer any question on her behalf. Zahra nodded to Noor's answer.

"How you liking it so far, love?" Iris continued.

"It is very good, I registered for the next semester too," Zahra answered.

When Noor left Diane's basement, Zahra wanted to leave with her, but Beth insisted that First Baptist had a contract with Diane that she expected Zahra to honor. Iris' house was on the opposite side of town and would have put Zahra much farther from school and work, so moving there was out of the question.

The first days without Noor were the hardest, especially since Zahra didn't have her phone yet. It was not until a week later that Beth showed up with "double good news," Zahra could register for a summer classes, and Wal-Mart called for her to start anytime. The weeks were a blur that started with an alarm waking her up at four in the morning and ended with falling asleep reading her class assignments.

Chapter Twenty-Seven

A month after she started working, Zahra got a phone and called Mustafa with her WhatsApp, which Noor helped her install. Mustafa cried the whole time they talked.

"*Shoo shtatilik ya,* Zahra!" He repeated how he missed her.

Zahra giggled and teased him about how his love life must not be very good, for him to miss her that much. He told her that he was renting his own space and using his own tools with the money she left for him. His salon was named "Roses." Mustafa named it after a flower, because Zahra meant "flower."

Mustafa had been dating a married man for the past month, and he seemed happy and in love.

"Victor is wonderful, he treats me like a prince!" Mustafa gushed. His boyfriend was Christian, he added, which, according to Mustafa, was a good thing because Victor was more liberated and fun.

Zahra reminded him about the heartache that came after Aziz, the last married man he dated, but Mustafa had forgotten the pain already. When he was in love, reason had to wait. He promised to text and call Zahra every day now that she had her own phone.

Zahra's calls and texts to Lebanon were free as long as she found a way to connect to the internet. Zahra figured out that standing outside McDonalds would allow her to use the internet. Wichita State, where she took her summer class, had internet too, but Zahra was usually running out of the class to catch the bus before it got too dark.

The busier Zahra got, the less she thought about going back to Lebanon. Her love for Nadim no longer felt like solitary confinement. Her heart seemed to be trading the solitary cell for a ball and chain, the chain grew a little longer every passing day. She had still not called him.

Every day she thought she was ready, and every day she stopped before she dialed his number. She rehearsed the conversation about her job, the summer classes, her new friends, and Hajji. She would tell him about Noor getting hurt but leave out some details. She would tell him about Iris but not about her daughter. Zahra hoped he would tell her about his life too, perhaps they could even talk about him visiting Wichita next summer.

When an unfamiliar number rang on Zahra's number she hoped it was Nadim. It turned out to be the surgeon's office in Kansas City confirming her appointment for the following Monday at quarter past eleven. Zahra had gone online at the student library, researched surgeons in the area, and requested an appointment on the website.

It was Beth's idea to "start looking for a doctor who could help." She asked Zahra about it every time they met. When Zahra finally ran out of excuses and looked, she realized that getting an appointment was not as impossible as she expected.

"I can take you to Kansas City. We can stop by our church and say hello to some of our friends!" Beth said that Friday afternoon, when she stopped by Diane's house. It was the day to give Diane the fifty dollars of rent from First Baptist office, to match the fifty Zahra paid. Beth seemed more interested in visiting Zahra after Noor left.

"I want to ask Noor if she can take me," Zahra said.

Beth's smile instantly disappeared and she nodded. Monday was Noor's day off and Zahra hoped Noor and Iris would take her to Kansas University for her consultation.

Zahra was scheduled to work Saturday and Sunday. She was in charge of stocking and inventory of the shelves and racks in the bay aisle at Wal-Mart. She spent her days emptying boxes that came from China. She arranged tiny folded clothes on shelves and hundreds of little dresses, shirts, shorts, and pants hangers. Baby sizes went up in three-month increment. After two years, it jumped one year at a time. This made as little sense to Zahra as the rest of the retail world of babies.

Diaper companies organized the diapers by weight, and the food companies seemed to focus on stages, whatever food stages were for kids. Zahra had cared for her nephews when she was a teenager, before her injury. What those babies ate then was mashed food from whatever the family cooked that day, and what they wore was something their older brothers had outgrown.

Mothers, grandmothers, and some fathers pushed kids around in carts while stocking up on baby formula, food, and clothes. She tried in vain to understand American's retail logic: people who seemed poor, unbathed, and tired filled up their cart with unnecessary toys, and formula. The richer a person looked, the less they piled up in their baskets. It was exactly the opposite of what she had seen in Lebanon where shopping was the privilege of the rich and breast-feeding a necessity for the poor.

What all the parents and grandparents of Wal-Mart had in common was their need for diapers—babies seemed to need those regardless what they wore, ate, or played with.

After her day of arranging colored food jars and teething rings, she hoped to visit Noor and Iris. She had still not told them about the appointment in Kansas City. Zahra thought about what could happen that Monday. She had spent the last ten years dreaming about undoing her injury. In two days, she would find out once and for all if it could be done.

When Zahra was eighteen, Nadim had taken her to a colorectal surgeon, someone who specializes in closing colostomies. The surgeon talked to Nadim as if Zahra was not in the room. He told Nadim that the risk in closing the colostomy was too high and that he advised against it.

Zahra cried for days after that visit, both for the loss of her dream and because Nadim didn't look at her once during the appointment to ask her what she wanted. This time she would speak and decide for herself.

That night Zahra called Noor to ask her about Monday. Noor got so excited, she screamed to Iris across the yard, "Go to Kansas City to close Zahra's colostomy!" Iris then ran to the house thinking that Noor was telling her Zahra already had the surgery. Iris grabbed the phone from Noor and was squealing and congratulating Zahra.

It took a few minutes for Zahra to explain to the two women that she didn't have the surgery yet and didn't even know if she could have it but that she wanted them to go find out with her.

"Of course we will go! I would never let you get surgery without being right there! Got to make sure those doctors don't mess something up!" Iris laughed, and Noor did too. Zahra could hear their giggles over the phone.

Their joy made her worry about disappointing them if the surgeon told her the same thing she had heard nine years ago.

When Zahra hung up, she turned off the star lamp that Noor left for her and closed her eyes. Sleep eluded her as thoughts of what might happen raced through her mind like fallen tree leaves in a storm. Mustafa was in love. She was not in Beirut to share his excitement, his anticipation, his dates, his wild nights, and then the tears that followed when the man moved on to another guy or became paranoid of getting caught.

Zahra wondered about love, what made it come to be, what melted it like snow.

She realized that she was in love with Nadim when she was still in the hospital. She noticed that her face became hot when he appeared in her hospital room, that her heart raced so fast she couldn't finish sentences. Love showed up one day after not being there the day before. Zahra kept hoping that it would disappear in a similar fashion. This was logic that she eventually gave up on.

When Nadim's voice reached her down the hospital hall, her insides tightened harder than with the worst cramps. She caught herself not breathing many days when he sat in a chair and told her stories. His scent lingered in the room long after he had been gone, his affectionate squeeze to her hand felt warm for days after it had ended. Nadim was fifteen years older than her, he treated her like a kid, loved her like a family member he felt responsible for. She didn't blame him for not desiring her, even when her groin throbbed for him. Mustafa was the only person who knew about Zahra's love for Nadim. Occasionally, Mustafa felt sorry for Zahra, especially when he was experiencing heartbreak himself, otherwise Zahra's love for Nadim was like her colostomy: an unfortunate fact Mustafa accepted without questions.

Chapter Twenty-Eight

Noor was tapping her feet on the blue carpet and biting her nails in the waiting room, while Iris read her romance novel. Zahra had gone into her appointment alone. She told them it was easier for her to hear what the doctor had to say without worrying about them. Every once in a while, Iris sighed. Noor was not sure if it was over the novel or out of worry for Zahra.

The drive to Kansas University Medical Center lasted over three hours. Noor packed snacks and had a three-hour long soundtrack. Iris brought her novel and read the "good parts" out loud. The main character in Iris's story was an officer in the Marines whose wife and son died in a boating accident. Afterward, he had sworn off love. When he meets his high school sweetheart, he desperately avoids falling in love with her *again*.

"But you know he won't be able to resist it! Not when that was the very first *and* biggest love of his life!" Iris explained this over the radio that played Noor's tunes.

Noor said that the Marine should, "Give it a test drive! See if he still enjoys the ride!" Then she laughed, but Iris got mad and told her she was "nasty." They both laughed, and Zahra smiled.

Her colostomy was acting up from her tense nerves, and they had to stop three times on the way. Iris and Noor were very sweet about it and not once complained. When the Marine got deployed in her story, Iris cried and said she was putting the book down.

The exam room was as plain as the rest of the building. It had an exam table on one end and two chairs upholstered in red on the other. In the middle of the room stood a black swiveling stool. The walls were white and above a small sink there were posters with drawings of bowels and colostomies. The room smelled of antiseptic and paper.

After a swift knock on the door, an exceptionally tall ginger-headed man in green scrubs entered. His eyebrows, eyelashes, and beard were a fierce, dark orange hue. He extended his hand towards Zahra and smiled.

"I am Doctor Knight, like the knight in shining armor!" The giant orange doctor laughed, and so did a tiny blond girl who carried a laptop and stood by the door.

The door opened again, and a woman with partly gray hair and blue eyes walked in. She was wearing purple scrubs.

"This is Jeanie, don't let her scare you! She will try hard!" The doctor reproduced his bellow-y laughter once more.

"Silly!" Jeanie said, looking at the doctor. Her eyes were kind. They reminded Zahra of the way Iris looked at her when she felt sorry for her.

Doctor Knight and the tiny girl, who turned out to be a resident or a doctor "learning to become a surgeon," listened to Zahra as she answered question after question about her injury. Zahra showed them the records of her one-year stay in the hospital. They were surprised that all Zahra's medical records were in English, which was good according to Doctor Knight. "Since there was not enough time today to learn Lebanese, that's your language, right?"

Zahra nodded; she didn't think explaining the fact that all Arabs spoke Arabic with one accent or the other was relevant to the visit. Zahra was too nervous to say much. Her heartbeat was in her throat and she worried those people might see it if she opened her mouth.

Nadim had given Zahra an envelope with her surgical report—the description of what happened in her surgery and studies showing what was left of Zahra's bowels. This was at her insistence. Nadim didn't think another surgery was a good idea. He advised Zahra to accept herself. She remained quiet until he stopped talking and never broached the subject again. Zahra wondered if anyone really ever "accepted" a colostomy. She thought what some people called "acceptance" was exhaustion and submission.

"My good golly! You are tougher than nails, young lady!" Doctor Knight said.

He explained to the tiny resident what he read and soon enough her expression matched his—a mix of disbelief and pity. Zahra's eyes were burning. Something about the doctor reading her surgical report made it real and reminded her of what she needed to forget.

"You are one lucky cat! Eight and a half lives later!" Doctor Knight announced, laughing.

The two women giggled with him. Zahra bit hard on her lip, until she tasted blood and it distracted her from how much she wanted to cry and yell at the doctor. He was joking about more pain than could fit in all his medical encyclopedias. She squinted her eyes and stared at the white linoleum.

"We can help you, young lady, I am pretty sure we can. It is going to take some studies, we need to check on your remaining bowels with a dye, something you drink, and we shoot films," he explained.

Zahra felt a dam break inside her heart. She cried harder than she had in a decade. Her tears tasted salty and warm. She smiled to the doctor and his helpers, and they smiled back.

When Zahra walked out back to the waiting room. Noor got up and walked towards her. Iris didn't see Zahra walking towards them. Zahra nodded to Noor and smiled.

"Eh? Eh?" Noor asked, wanting to know what was going on.

"*Momkin*," Zahra said. It was possible, that was all she knew, all she needed and wanted to know.

Noor let out a joyful scream that sent Iris' book onto the blue carpet. Iris looked up to Noor hugging Zahra and crying and she followed suit. Patients and their families in the waiting room looked at the three women hugging and crying.

"He asks her to marry him!" Iris said, as she picked up her book and hit Noor on the head with it.

Chapter Twenty-Nine

Zahra moved out of Diane's basement on a Sunday morning, almost four years after she moved in. It was a cool and sunny spring day. The trees along the entire block of the new apartment were covered with blooms; pinks, purples and whites quivered in harmony with the wind. Noor and Iris helped her, and so did Zahra's closest friends, Joel and Emily, from the philosophy club at the university.

It turned out some people had read the same books and formed similar thoughts oceans away from Beirut. Zahra had gotten better at reading English and understanding it, she sometimes even dreamt in it.

They used Joel's truck to move a bed, a love seat, and a dinette set that Noor found for Zahra at the thrift store.

"A couple spray paint cans and some fabric will turn this furniture to designer pieces! Design by Noor!" Noor said. She told everyone where everything should be placed, as Iris and Zahra rolled their eyes. Noor had drawn a sketch of what the apartment would look like furnished. She showed Zahra pictures on her phone that looked pretty good, better than any place she had lived or thought she would ever live in.

The crew of five people worked all day until the one-bedroom apartment was ready. Zahra's bedroom was painted a light sky blue. It worked well with the star lamp and the bedspread that Zahra got at Wal-Mart for twenty dollars with her employee discount. She had been the employee of the month twice in the time she worked at Wal-Mart, and her supervisor told her a raise would happen next, a whole extra dollar per hour.

Zahra had already decided that she was going to start working at the nursing home where she volunteered a couple times a month. Being around elders comforted her, and made Hajji seem not so far away. She could bike to her new job from her apartment, and the university was also a ten-minute bike ride away. Bike rides were Zahra's favorite thing to do, since Iris gave her a bike that "was done sitting in the garage and needed places to go."

Zahra had finished enough credits at WSU to graduate one semester early with honors with a Bachelor's in Sociology and Social Work.

On the coffee table sat a frame with a picture of Nadim and Hajji. Zahra dreamt of Hajji one night. In Zahra's dream, Hajji's eyes were not confused, she told Zahra to fly. Zahra tried in vain to explain to Hajji that she didn't have wings. When she woke up, Zahra called Nadim.

"Hajji died this morning," he said, "I was going to call you when everybody left." Zahra told him that she wanted to go back for Hajji's funeral, Nadim told her to stay in Wichita. "You will not make it in time for her funeral, she will be buried before sunset."

Zahra cried, and Nadim cried with her. She wrote a letter to him that night, told him that she had been in love with him for almost half her life and that she needed to know if he felt the same way about her.

She didn't get a reply for months. When she finally did, he told her that he didn't love her in the way she deserved to be loved, that he suspected her love for a long time. He asked her to forgive him for not telling her sooner that he was not in love with her.

"Keeping you in the dark only made things worse," he wrote. Zahra wrote back to him, and said:

"Love is a wild animal trapped in humans' hearts, no man or god to date has been able to tame it, it would be vain of me to try. Whether I live or die, meet someone or stay alone, the fact remains that love will always look like you. If there is a God, I ask Him to keep you safe and happy and to make you take up a little less room in my heart every day."

That was her goodbye to him, the last time she allowed herself in her waking hours to think about Nadim. He never stopped visiting her in her dreams; she in a hospital bed and him across the room in a chair discussing everything under the stars.

Zahra bought pizza for her helpers as they sat in her living room with a downtown view. On one end Zahra saw Wichita State University, and on the other stood the tall building where, a little over three years ago, she was shining clean mirrors and windows with Noor. Zahra looked at Noor to see if she remembered the building, but Noor was not paying attention to Zahra. Noor's pretty smile was directed at Joel.

Iris was telling everyone how Noor just got her new driver's license in the mail.

"Show them!" Iris ordered.

A smiling, blushing Noor pulled a laminated rectangle with her photo flashing her big white teeth. Next to sex was an *F,* underneath which "*Noor Iris Hadi*" had signed her name.

Joel's hand brushed against Noor's when he handed her license back. Noor looked down and Joel did too. Zahra felt happy tears in her eyes and a lightness exactly where her colostomy used to be.